Helen and Frank

Getting Older and Finding Love with Food, Wine, Theater, Music, Crime and COVID

THOMAS MORGAN

TMH Books

ISBN (print): 978-1-7376747-0-2
ISBN (e-book): 978-1-393096-3-68

Cover Design: Jodi Parrish

10 9 8 7 6 5 4 3 2 1
First edition 2021

TMH Books
St. Louis, MO

DEDICATION

To Older People Everywhere

ACKNOWLEDGEMENT

The author thanks Tom Hunter, Adam Hyers, Gail Roberts, Gerald Roberts, and Anne Williams for helpful comments after reading all or parts of this story.

Introduction

The viral infection we know as Covid-19 has been the defining event of 2020, perhaps the defining event of our lifetimes. We have no personal experience of the influenza pandemic of 1918-1921. We can only hear and read about it. My father was an 18-year-old U.S. Army recruit when he contracted that virulent strain of influenza in 1918. He told me much later that it was the worst malady he had ever experienced. By the time he recovered, World War I was over, and he was discharged to civilian life. The death toll from that pandemic has been estimated at 50 million lives worldwide. There were no antivirals, vaccines, monoclonal antibodies, ventilators or intensive care units available then. Infusion of convalescent plasma from recovered patients was the only treatment available beyond supportive care. Contact tracing, quarantines, masks, and social distancing probably greatly reduced the death toll then. That pandemic ran through several waves but was largely over by 1921 because of widespread immunity in the population—so-called herd immunity.

Like influenza, Covid-19 is a contagious viral disease that spreads mainly in the air we exhale. Unlike influenza, which kills the very young and very old, Covid-19 mainly kills older people. We have quickly developed treatments, vaccines, and public health initiatives against Covid-19, but missteps have abounded. Our political and scientific leaders at first downplayed the danger and then overreacted. Lockdowns were too draconian. Unproven treatments and preventatives were touted. Infected people were sent to nursing homes after hospital discharge. Vaccine critics were given too much credibility. Our 'experts' vacillated and then acted as if they understood everything about the new virus. Humility has been in short supply.

On a personal level, the disease has disheartened older people. Growing old is often an ordeal, but the thought of being stalked by Covid-19 adds untold fear and anxiety to that ordeal. Institutionalized older people have been especially vulnerable. We can estimate the death toll from Covid-19, and we can count suicides among the anxious and depressed population. Counting the people whose health deteriorated because of inability to seek medical care is more difficult. We know that the lockdowns have been a huge financial, social and emotional burden, but it is difficult to put numbers on this burden.

Frank Palermo in this story lived in a memory support complex in 2020. From March to September of 2020, Frank basically was confined to his apartment. His food was brought to him, and his trash was hauled away. He was lucky in that he could still drive his car, but where could he go? Restaurants, theaters, concerts and other entertainment venues were unavailable to him. He was prohibited from group meals and other forms of socialization with residents in his complex. Frank had the internet as his primary form of communication and education. It was the way he experienced the world for almost six months. His confinement made Frank a stronger person, but to many older people the enforced isolation became unbearable. Helen, a penniless widow, moved into Frank's complex in September and changed his life. The story of *Helen and Frank* aims to put a human face on the extraordinary year of 2020.

"From now on it can be said that plague was the concern of all of us."

\- Part 2 of *The Plague* by Albert Camus

CHAPTER 1

Frank Palermo's grandfather had warned him long ago about getting old, but some truths must be experienced to be understood. Now Frank had grown old, and the year 2020 was the worst time he could remember. As if being old were not enough, a deadly virus was targeting old people. The combination of a forced confinement in his apartment for six months and a deadly virus stalking him made Frank's life miserable. He lived at Beaumont Life Terrace Retirement Community, a complex that had been constructed in 2000 in an unincorporated part of south St. Louis County. A rapidly aging population living nearby was the impetus. Beaumont's sales pitch, 'It's Not Retirement, It's the Best Time of Your Life,' featured a premium experience with gourmet food, luxurious furnishings, and a socially active lifestyle. Unfortunately, over the next twenty years, the owners had done little to refurbish the complex. The older population in the area had either died or moved to the Sunbelt, and younger couples with children had moved in, looking for better jobs and schools in the suburbs. Beaumont had devolved into a memory care facility with housing gradations ranging from independent living to a fully secure dementia unit.

September first of 2020 found Francesco Cabrini Palermo and Charles Jessie Johnson seated beside the little pond that was Beaumont's single piece of outdoor landscaping. The pond featured a statue of Hebe, the Roman goddess of youth, at its center. Hebe, like much of Beaumont, had fallen into disrepair during the pandemic lockdown, and she no longer spewed water from her mouth to aerate the pond. She had recently been repaired after repeated requests from the residents, and now the pond water was clear, attracting ducks and geese again.

"It's great to be out here, Charlie. I've missed the ducks. I've even missed the squirrels that try to steal the duck food."

"The lockdown was grim," Charlie said. "I was going stir-crazy in my apartment. About the only thing I could do was drink and gamble."

Luckily for its occupants, Beaumont staff had carefully screened new residents during the six-month lockdown, and visitors were strictly limited. Covid-19 did not take as devastating a toll at Beaumont as had happened in other communal living facilities. Unluckily for the occupants, the rigid lockdown deprived them of nearly all social contact. Possibly because of these measures, only two fatal cases of Covid-19 had occurred at Beaumont. This allowed the owners of Beaumont and the county authorities to boast that the lockdown had been a success. They failed to mention the three suicides that had also occurred there during the same six months.

"I'm glad young Hebe is working again," Frank said as he threw more feed at the ducks.

"There's a cruel irony to putting a goddess of youth in a dump like this. I think the owners were trying to sell this place when the virus hit."

Charlie remembered little about irony. He held a paper cup of Scotch and had a small bottle in his coat pocket. He planned to replenish their hidden supply of contraband liquor in the library when he got the chance. Charlie wanted his life to return to normal and that included trying to seduce the secretaries in the business office with alcohol. Residents were finally being allowed out of their apartments and back into common areas and seated for dinner in the dining room. Social distancing was enforced, and masks were required except when eating.

"Frank, sometimes I wonder if you don't belong here. You're too smart to live in a memory unit."

Frank smiled and asked himself the same question. He didn't mention that Charlie was one reason for his continued stay at Beaumont. They had become friends out of necessity, being two of the more functional men at Beaumont. Frank liked Charlie and looked out for him.

They both heard and felt Barney the nursing aide approaching behind them. Barney was so massive that you could sense his approach before you saw him. He was their single friend on the staff—a reliable supplier of liquor and marijuana from the outside.

"I know you dudes are glad to be out of lockdown," Barney said. "I think your chances are looking up in general. There's a new resident moving in, and she's a real mamma. That means gorgeous to you, Frank. She already asked about you."

Later that afternoon, Charlie found Frank reading in the library. "You seen the new girl yet?" he asked.

"The new resident Barney was talking about?" Frank said.

"She moved into three-twelve—the two-bedroom unit. She's easy on the eyes. Application says she's seventy-five, but she can't be a day over sixty."

"Well, we can use some scenic improvement around here."

"You'll see her at dinner. Application says her name is Helen Corbett ... from Denver"

Frank did see her in the lounge before dinner, and for once Charlie had not exaggerated. She approached to within six feet and clearly smiled behind her mask. "Hello," she said, "I'm Helen Corbett."

Soft dinner music was playing over the public address system. It was the old favorite "Heart and Soul." Frank had been listening, and Helen had lifted him from his reverie.

"Welcome to TLC. I'm Frank Palermo," he replied.

She fixed azure eyes on him. "TLC?"

Frank felt a stirring somewhere between his gut and his groin—a feeling he had almost forgotten. "It's shorthand for what we call this place. Want to join us in the library for a drink?"

"I was told no alcohol is served in the common areas."

"Charlie and I keep a few bottles behind the dictionaries and Bibles. Nobody ever looks there. We use them to tempt women into sin and corruption."

"I can already tell that you and this Charlie are the troublemakers in this place."

"We're not troublemakers, just realists."

They walked into the library and introductions were made. Helen said she had moved from Denver after her husband died. She told them she had a nephew in St. Louis. They exchanged brief life histories, but Helen seemed to be focused on Frank. Charlie gave them paper cups of Scotch and wandered back to the lounge.

"You don't remember me, do you?" she asked.

"I remember the last time I saw you, you weren't wearing a mask."

Helen laughed. "I can imagine that. My husband and I came to your restaurant about ten years ago. You walked by in your whites. You were very handsome."

"I always tried to walk through the dining room at least twice every night. I got the pulse of the place by doing that."

"Never mind. I remember you. So, how's this place working out for you?"

"It's not perfect, I admit, but I like it, I guess. I'd move out, but then Covid happened. My nephew in Chicago says I need to stay here. My doctors tell me I have something called mild cognitive impairment. They ran a bunch of tests on me, and that's what they came up with."

"My doctors tell me I have the same thing."

"You don't look it."

"You can't tell by looking at me. I have trouble remembering things, and I get mad and I can't remember why I got mad. It's embarrassing."

"Don't worry. You'll fit right in here. The inmates out here are pretty much functional. We're lucky we aren't on the locked ward. That's where you don't want to be."

"What do you do with your spare time? And don't tell me you spend all your time in the library."

"I study the markets, and I invest," Frank said.

Helen's eyes smiled. "I'll bet you don't know much about money."

"I do okay. I ran a successful restaurant for over thirty-five years."

"Alright. What's the difference between a stock and a bond?"

"That's easy. A stock is a possibility; a bond is a promise."

"Oh...so you're a poet."

"No. I'm a realist. I understand things. A stock is also a pricing mechanism."

"So...you like money."

"Of course I like money. I'm a realist."

Frank felt himself running out of clever patter. Beautiful women had always done that to him, and every part of Helen had clearly resisted the stress of time. She was what Frank's late wife, Angela, would have called 'well-preserved.' But it was her blue eyes that drew him in. Those eyes seemed to change tint with sun and shadow. Frank found it difficult to look into her eyes and talk at the same time.

"Tell me about your restaurant," Helen said.

"It was a simple place. We had Italian food—steaks, chops, pasta. We made strong drinks and had good wine at decent prices. It was popular."

"It must have been a gold mine."

"We did okay."

"Please forgive me for asking. Who is we?"

"My wife and me. Angie passed away about five years ago. After she passed, the fire in me seemed to go out. I sold it and moved in here. It's still there. I'll take you to dinner if you like."

"You drive?"

"I have a car and a license. Yeah."

"I'd like that if you promise not to have an accident."

The friendship between the two men and Helen grew quickly, lubricated by afternoon alcohol and Helen's evident interest in Frank. Her interest was a welcome diversion for Frank, although Charlie did not seem that impressed with her. Frank thought maybe he was a little jealous. Charlie had always been the one who attracted women, even in Beaumont. The two men had never reconciled themselves to living in a memory care unit. They had not made many friends other than Charlie's conquests in the business office, and they both viewed the staff, with the exception of Barney, as guards rather than helpers. Helen, in contrast, immediately threw herself into the life of Beaumont, joining several women's groups and working out in the tiny gym. She was friendly to the other women residents and eager to help with their personal needs and memory difficulties.

A few days later, Frank took her to dinner at Palermos, his old restaurant. As soon as they walked in, the new owner greeted them. "Frank, *mio amico*, how are you? Long time no see. And who is this lovely lady with you?"

Frank responded with an awkward silence. Helen stepped up and introduced herself. "I'm Helen Corbett. I'm new at Beaumont, and Frank tells me this is the place to eat around here."

"If it is, it was because of Angie, not Frank. Frank took all the credit, but Angie made the whole thing work, from the kitchen, to the table service, to the business end. Let me get you settled, and I'll bring you some Prosecco."

When they were seated, she glared at him. "Why didn't you introduce me?"

"I'm sorry...I forgot his name. I seem to remember names after it's too late to do any good. I haven't been here in a long time."

"Oh, for the love of... oh, never mind. All you have to remember is my name."

After another awkward silence, Helen said, "I have to ask you. Why didn't you put an apostrophe in Palermos?"

Frank laughed. "You must be an English major. When we first started the restaurant, the neon sign guy wanted double the price to put the apostrophe in our name. We just said forget it, and it's been this way ever since.'

Frank was silent again. Finally, Helen said, "Restaurant owner, investor, market analyst. There's more to you than I know. And I would like to know more."

"I'm Francis Cabrini Palermo. There's a Xavier in there on the birth certificate, but I don't use it."

"It certainly is an interesting name."

My mother wanted to crowd in as many saints as she could. We're Sicilian. I'm second generation. I've been in the restaurant business all my life. Started as a busboy and worked my way up. Angie was from Lombardy, near Milano...that's Milan. Sicilian soul and Lombardy brains and know-how, you know what I mean?"

"What did you do for fun?"

"We traveled some—mostly back to Italy. Angie had family in Lombardy, and I had cousins in Sicily—mostly my nephew's family. A restaurant is a full-time business. If you aren't around, everything that's valuable gets legs and walks out the door. Steaks, booze, and cash— everything that's portable."

"So…you met in Italy?"

"No, we met here. Angie came here as an exchange student at my high school. We hit it off right away. She thought I was handsome, and I knew she was the smartest person I'd ever met. After she went back to Italy we stayed in touch. Her family didn't like me much, being Sicilian, but I kept after her. Eventually we got married, and she moved back here. We were living in an Italian area called The Hill."

"I know about The Hill. It's an old Italian neighborhood that goes back a long time."

"Anyway, I was working in a restaurant there, and Angie saw it as a dead-end job. We saved some money and started a little restaurant together in south county. I cooked, and Angie worked the front and kept the books. With her involved it became very successful."

"Children?"

"No… that was a big disappointment to us."

"I know what you mean. We had no children either."

"I'm telling you all about me. What about you?"

"I told you my husband died when we were living in Denver. He was an investor and entrepreneur, and he was good at it. Now my only family is a nephew here in St. Louis. Jeffrey insisted I move here so he can keep an eye on me. He doesn't think I should be living independently."

CHAPTER 2

Palermos Restaurant became a meeting place for the three friends, although Charlie seemed increasingly reluctant to join them. He could see that Helen was interested in Frank, and he began to beg off when invited. The threesome became a twosome that gathered at the restaurant to escape the bland food at Beaumont and to have some quiet time together. Frank usually ordered pasta and Helen liked the fish. Frank told her that the profit margins weren't good on fish, but you had to serve good fish to appeal to women. Pasta, steaks, and alcohol were where you made your money.

Frank grew interested in Helen's story and wanted to know more about her late husband's business. Helen was vague about her past and seemed only interested in Frank's story. Finally, in response to his persistence, she suggested they dine with her nephew. She said her nephew could explain the business, and she arranged for them to meet him over dinner.

When they next gathered at Palermos, Helen introduced her nephew as Jeffrey Maddox. He looked to be about forty—an exceptionally well-groomed and dressed man—who projected competence but not arrogance. Frank didn't like his looks, but Jeffrey had a convincing way of calling attention to his business plans, not to himself.

"We're really excited about it," he said. "It's a cloud-based package that will do everything for business—spreadsheets, analysis, payroll, tax preparation, messaging—every app you could want or need."

"Aren't there already programs for that stuff?"

"Not like this. And it's user friendly—very easy to navigate with features that let you modify it on the fly. It's also very hard to hack into. We're working on including video conferencing now. It will appeal to both small and large businesses."

"Why haven't I heard about it?"

"It's in development. We had it just about ready to launch when Uncle Henry died. At that point our financing slowed down because Uncle Henry was the public face of the effort. When it's finished, we think it will be better than anything Microsoft or anybody else has out there.

"Take a look at this," Jeffrey continued. He placed a small laptop on the table, fired up a program, and quickly scrolled through some spreadsheet and messaging applications. "This software will be able to do anything."

Frank wasn't sure he understood what Jeffrey was saying, but he was impressed. In all the years at their restaurant, Angie had done the books by hand until near the end when she had tried a business software package and decided she didn't like it. Frank knew that her decision may have been influenced by her general dislike of computers. An inner voice told Frank to be careful, but he also knew how valuable a software package like this could be to a small business. The dinner passed without a further sales pitch from Jeffrey. The young man didn't seem interested in Frank's involvement, but Helen kept up a subtle encouragement about the investment possibilities.

Frank was intrigued. When he returned to Beaumont, he looked up Henry Corbett on the internet and found an obituary for a Henry Corbett in Denver, who had died about a year earlier. Corbett was described as an investor in start-up companies in the Denver and Northern California areas. He had apparently been successful, according to the obituary. His wife, Helen Corbett, was listed as a survivor along with two sons from a previous marriage.

Other dinner meetings with Jeffrey followed. In response to Frank's inquiries, the young man slowly laid out the business plan for the software package. During this interval, Helen paid even more attention to Frank. One night when the two dined together, she suggested that Frank come back to her apartment for a nightcap. They each had two glasses of wine with dinner, and when they returned to her apartment, Helen served more wine. When she nestled beside him on the couch, Frank kissed her. He thought her breath was sweet. He kissed her again. Helen took his hand and led him into her bedroom. They undressed each other and tumbled into her bed. Frank decided that she was beyond 'well preserved,' she was almost physically perfect. He tried to tell her, but she pressed a finger to his lips.

"Don't talk," she said. "Just hold me. I am so lonely."

They held each other, and she proceeded to please him with her hands. Her hands were more skillful than Frank had ever experienced or imagined. He was passive at first, but with her encouragement, he began to explore her. They spent three hours in bed before she said it was getting late. He dressed and she slipped on a robe and led him to the door.

"I'm afraid I'm just plain vanilla, not fancy or razzle-dazzle. I haven't been with a woman in a long time."

"I've done fancy and razzle-dazzle. I'm ready for plain vanilla." Helen kissed him and pushed him out the door.

Frank had not felt the ardor of a woman for over a decade. Angie had been sick with cancer for the last five years of her life, and Frank had lived like a monk for five years since her death. He had forgotten the touch, warmth, and smell of holding a beautiful woman. He slept better that night than he had in years.

Other meetings with Jeffrey followed, interspersed with evenings with Helen in her apartment. After two weeks, Frank had overcome his doubts, and he wrote a check to Jeffrey for one hundred thousand dollars. Both Helen and Jeffrey expressed surprise that Frank could produce so much money, but Jeffrey accepted the check and assured him that this investment would get the software prepared for its public launch.

One afternoon after Frank's investment in the software venture, Charlie was sitting in the library pretending to read a book when Frank walked in and said, "They can scrub this place down as much as they want, it still smells like urine."

"I don't smell anything," Charlie said.

"You got that right, buddy, and you don't remember anything either."

Charlie had no rebuttal. "Frank," he said, "I need to talk to you about Helen."

Frank waited for Charlie to continue. "I'm sorry and this will probably piss you off, but something's not right about her. First of all, she's too smart and rich for this place. I checked her application—says she's worth five million and has a trust fund. You see how she dresses."

"Charlie, you've got inside information. You've been after that new secretary in the business office."

"So what? She needs comfort, and I'm here to give it to her. My brains aren't so hot, but I still work from the neck down."

Charlie, if we combined ourselves, we'd be a complete man."

"I'm not kidding; you need to be careful."

"Okay, my friend, your reservations are noted. I'll be on the lookout."

"You're falling for her, aren't you?"

"I like her. She's nice to me and we can talk about stuff I usually don't talk about."

"Frank, I've seen her walking around outside talking on her cellphone. She looks like she's on top of her game to me."

"I hear you."

"Just be careful," Charlie said. "By the way, you seen my cellphone?"

"Buddy, I have trouble finding my own phone. Just pick up the house phone and call your cell. That's how I find mine."

"That's no good. I keep it turned off. I don't want people calling me."

***

Also, around the time of Frank's big investment, Vincenzo Alessandro Palermo, Frank's nephew, was sitting at his desk in the Hancock Building in Chicago when two of his accountants came in for a scheduled appointment. "Mr. Palermo," said one, "It has come to our attention that your Uncle Frank is drawing significant amounts out of your joint account in St. Louis."

"Tell me more," Vinnie said.

"Well, he's frequently spending time at his old restaurant down there. He always seems to be with the same woman. We have identified her as a new resident at Beaumont named Helen Corbett. Just this week he drew down the account by a hundred thousand dollars."

Vinnie was temporarily stunned. "All at once? What did he do with the money?"

"We don't know, sir. It was a cashier's check made out to a Jeffrey Maddox."

"Why didn't you tell me about this earlier?"

"We're sorry, sir. It's all so uncharacteristic for him that by the time we had confirmed the numbers, it had gotten out of control like this."

Vinnie made a mental note to fire both accountants. "I need to talk to Uncle Frank. Find out if we can video conference with him. It will have to be in his apartment."

"We anticipated that, sir. He has video conference capability in his apartment. We set it up for this afternoon at two. Your schedule is open at that time."

"Good. And find out who this Helen Corbett is and this Jeffrey Maddox. Something's not right in St. Louis."

When Vinnie and Frank had their video meeting that afternoon, Frank was very proactive. He told Vinnie that he had an investment deal going that was already sealed and delivered—a business software package like no other.

"Frank, you wrote that big check to a person, this Maddox guy. How do you know where that money went?"

"Vinnie, this is on the level. I've seen some of this software work. I'll send you the business plan."

Vinnie was skeptical. "You're spending a lot of money, Frank, and it's my money. I didn't set up this account for you to invest. I only made it a joint account to give you a little more financial freedom. Maybe I should come down there. I think we need to discuss this face-to-face."

"Please don't do that, Vinnie. With the pandemic, it's too risky for both of us. I swear this deal is done. There won't be more withdrawals. You'll begin to see a return on this investment very soon."

"I can take my plane to Spirit Airport and take a car down to your place. I won't use public transportation. It'll be a low-risk trip. I want to talk to this Maddox guy."

Frank's real motivation was that he didn't want Vinnie to see the tattered condition of Beaumont. "It's really not necessary. I'll send you the business plan for the package. I won't do any more withdrawals. I think you'll be really pleased with what I'm doing. Just give it a little time."

Vinnie made no travel plans after more reassurance from Frank, but he was worried about his bank account in St. Louis—his plan B escape money.

Frank feared that Vinnie might show up unannounced. He knew Vinnie's capability.

CHAPTER 3

Frank decided that he really liked Helen. She looked at him when he talked and seemed genuinely interested in what he had to say. She was certainly pretty, but there was something about the way she held herself that impressed him. She was short in stature, but she carried herself in a way that made you think she was taller. He was also intrigued with a past that she seemed reluctant to divulge. One night at Palermos, he prodded her about her previous life, and she only told him what she had already shared—her late husband had been the lead investor on a nearly completed business office software package. She thought it would be revolutionary, that it would dominate its software segment, but he had already heard that from Jeffrey. The mystery and potential wealth of the software package only served to heighten Frank's interest.

They were eating at Palermos almost every night. The new owner always put them in an alcove off the main dining room where they had some privacy. They had tried other restaurants in the area, but they always came back to Palermos. The food at Beaumont held no attraction although it was included with the monthly residence fee. During another evening, she asked him about his travels in Italy, and he was only too happy to tell her. Italy and its food were two of his favorite subjects.

"Our restaurant was not fancy. There are many really good Italian restaurants in St. Louis, but they're mostly high-end places for special occasions. We tried to do the little things right. Two things Angie insisted on from the beginning were cold salad plates and clean bathrooms."

Helen smiled and waited for him to continue. When she smiled without her mask, her eyes were even more attractive and encouraging to Frank. "We served good homemade pasta and sauces at reasonable prices. Our marinara sauce was basic—brown anchovies, good olive oil, and fresh tomatoes—with just enough chopped garlic. A little sugar to finish it and don't overcook it. It went on anything. Our customers loved it. We also had tomato-basil and white wine with garlic available. That was it on our sauces unless a good customer made a special request. I'll tell you how we made our meatballs, but we'll have to be better friends before I do that."

"Pizza?"

"Oh yeah. We did a lot of that. Pizza with the very thin crust—St. Louis style. Many Americans don't like the more rustic Italian style. We made our own pizza, but we had to make it look like it came from the supermarket. Otherwise, the kids wouldn't eat it."

"Where did you go in Italy?"

"My uncle's family had a summer place on Salina. It's a little island north of Sicily. It's famous for growing capers. They have good wine there too. I would go there for long visits in the summer as a kid. Angie and I went there once after we got married, but she didn't like it—said it was too hot. I think part of it was she didn't like some of my relatives."

"Where did she like to go?"

"She liked Perugia and Le Marche. That's in the middle. You can get there on a fast train from Rome or Milan. Remember she was from Milan. We'd go to Perugia for a few days sampling the food and wine. Most of what they served didn't transfer well to our restaurant, but it was fun to know where the high end of Italian food and wine was going. Then we'd drive over to the Adriatic coast along Le Marche. They have the best seafood in Italy, and the tourists mostly don't go there. They don't know about it."

"Was there anywhere else she liked to go?"

"She didn't like crowds. We had enough of that in the restaurant every night. So that ruled out the big tourist attractions in Italy. No, it was Perugia and Le Marche where she liked to go. Her family loved it too. They had a place on the coast near Ancona. Angie would go there every summer as a kid. There's a really good restaurant in Ancona. Much finer food than anything we served—better than just about any restaurant anywhere."

"I don't know much about Italy."

Frank could tell Helen was growing uncomfortable talking about Angie. "You'd love Italy," he said. "I'll take you there when this pandemic lets up. It's beautiful, and the people are very friendly. Italy has the best food, wine, and style you'll find anywhere. They just can't seem to govern themselves. They have some of the most sophisticated corruption you'll find anywhere, too."

"I'd love to go to Italy with you and see some of those places. But I'd be afraid we'd be accompanied by a ghost."

"A ghost?"

"I mean Angie. I would feel like I was walking in her footsteps."

Frank thought about her comment. She had led him into talking about Angie, and now she seemed to want him to discount his history with his late wife. He would never disparage Angie's memory, but Helen was becoming important to him. He found himself thinking about Angie less every day. He was ready to tell Helen how important she was to him when their food arrived. Helen set into her fish and Frank into his linguine *tutto mare*. The arrival of their food saved Frank from having to tell Helen that he was falling hard for her.

Jeffrey occasionally joined them for dinner—Frank trying to pull business details out of him, and Jeffrey acting like he didn't care. Jeffrey assured Frank that his first investment had brought the software package well along toward its launch. The young man seemed certain that he could obtain more financing if needed.

Frank was becoming impatient. He couldn't understand why they hadn't launched the software. He wanted to get the ball rolling on this deal—make some real money and get Vinnie off his back. "Are you sure you can get the financing?" he asked. "I can help out if it will speed things up."

"It's not just financing. We have to debug the software. The worst thing we could do is put out an inferior product."

"What do you need for that? More programmers?"

"Programmers and skilled businesspeople to troubleshoot the software. People who can run complex business scenarios to find flaws in the software. You can't find people like that on every street corner. We're also incorporating video conferencing into the package. It will be the complete deal when we're done."

"If it's just money, I can—"

"Let me think about it," Jeffrey interrupted.

Jeffrey's seeming indifference to Frank's enthusiasm only made him more determined to invest additional money. Frank saw this as a ground-floor chance at a great investment and a way to convince his nephew Vinnie that his old uncle was still in the game. He began to research business software on the internet. He looked at Microsoft and Intuit and then checked out some of the newcomers, including Salesforce and Slack. He found it all confusing. Angie had taken care of the business end of the restaurant's operations. She did it all including their tax returns, which she would give to him only to sign. Yet, he knew that a comprehensive business software package had to be valuable. Angie had often complained about the drudgery of this work. At the same time his naturally cautious mind told him to proceed carefully.

One night at Palermos, Jeffrey said, "The skilled people we need to run the beta tests on our software are in short supply and they have to be paid. The people we thought we had lined up have all been hired away from us since Salesforce bought Slack. It's a seller's market out there with these technical people, believe me."

"I read about that purchase," Frank said.

"We also need more specialized programmers for the video conferencing and messaging capabilities. If you want to make another investment, I think it will speed things up."

Frank was excited despite his inherent caution. "How much do you need?"

"I don't want to stress you financially. How much can you spare?"

"Tell me how much you need. I want to get this package done and on the market."

"How about three or four hundred thousand?" Jeffrey didn't seem to think that was much money. "Is that possible for you? Otherwise, I can go to some of our investors in California."

"It's Wednesday. Meet me here tomorrow night, and I'll give you the check. I want to get this product out there."

On Thursday when they met for dinner, Frank handed Jeffrey a cashier's check for four hundred thousand dollars. He told Jeffrey that he wanted an ownership agreement for profit sharing, and Jeffrey replied that he would put an agreement together. He pressed Jeffrey for an estimate of when the finished product would be on the market, but the young man only replied that patience was a virtue at this point. The software package would soon be ready to market and that it would be a blockbuster. He also hinted that he had additional investors lined up to promote the package once it was on the market.

CHAPTER 4

Vinnie thought his uncle's prodigal behavior was finished. Then one of his assistants informed him that an additional four hundred thousand dollars had changed hands. "What the hell is he thinking? Is he thinking at all? I thought this thing was done. You'd better bring him up here." Vinnie's mind was a little agitated. "And don't send any of our goons. I love my uncle, but he's in over his head this time—giving money to strangers like this. He and Aunt Angie helped me when I was a kid. They took care of me when my parents died. Send our good people."

Frank had no desire to travel to Chicago, but Vinnie's people were insistent. At precisely six a.m. on October fifteenth, a man in a black sedan met Frank at the entrance to Beaumont. The driver didn't say much on the way to Spirit Airport except to express his concern that the early morning trip was not too much trouble for Frank. When they arrived at the airport, the man walked him through security to Vinnie's jet and handed him over to a smiling flight attendant. At Midway Airport, another man in a dark suit met him outside private aviation security and led him to another black sedan. The Chicago driver also had little to say. When they arrived downtown at the Hancock Building, a third man in a dark suit met the car and took him to Vinnie's office suite on the twentieth floor.

It was a busy office with multiple secretaries working at computer terminals and answering phones. Frank could see several glass-walled conference rooms occupied by earnest young people, who appeared to be thoroughly engaged in their work. Their work areas were separated by clear plastic partitions when possible, and everyone was masked and properly distanced. When Vinnie's assistant showed Frank into the large corner suite, the nephew embraced him, kissed his cheek, and pointed to a chair. The assistant offered refreshment, which Frank declined. He realized that Vinnie was the first person he'd encountered in months who did not practice social distancing and wondered if his nephew had already caught the virus.

Vinnie joined him in another chair in front of the massive desk. "Frank," he said, "let's get down to it. My finance people are telling me you've made another even larger withdrawal from our joint account."

Frank took off his mask. "Vinnie, I'm in on a really good thing. It's a business software package that will do everything. It's just about ready for release."

"You will remember I created this joint account as an insurance policy for me, not for you to invest. I only set it up as a joint account to make your life a little easier. I never thought you'd be taking this much money out of it."

"I know, but this thing could really take off—make us both rich."

"I'm already rich, Frank."

"I mean really rich."

"Frank, I'm already really rich. Let me ask you something. Do you know who this Helen Corbett is? Her real name is Helen Cohen. She's an actress from Omaha...done regional theater out there for thirty years."

"She told me she was from Denver."

"The Denver connection is a total sham. Helen Cohen has assumed Helen Corbett's identity. The real Helen Corbett is now living in a nursing home in Seattle. She moved there after her husband died. The husband, Henry Corbett, had no connection to this woman you're seeing. Helen Cohen's real husband sold real estate in Omaha. He died about the same time Henry Corbett did. What I'll bet your new girlfriend didn't tell you is she had two husbands before that—and two divorces."

Frank sat in angry silence. He knew his nephew too well to doubt what he was saying. Vinnie had lawyers, investigators, and other connections feeding him information that other people couldn't get.

"They're setting you up, Frank. The so-called nephew is a small-time grifter. He's also a talented forger. He's known this Cohen woman for years. He's in St. Louis now. He must have found out about my bank account."

"You're sure?"

Vinnie handed him a neatly bound file. "It's all in the file. They're already into you for half a million. They'll ask you for more and then disappear."

Frank leafed through the file. He scanned information on Helen's two divorces and her theatrical career in Omaha. Both of his checks were now deposited in a Cayman Islands bank and credited to a limited liability corporation that Frank didn't recognize. He was embarrassed and angry, but he knew he had to placate Vinnie. "I'm sorry, Vinnie. I thought the money would put me in on the ground floor of a big idea."

Vinnie took back the file. "It's my money, Frank, and I want it back."

"Please don't hurt her."

"My branch of the outfit up here doesn't work that way anymore. Whack jobs and car bombs are out of style—poor salesmanship. There's too much money to be made in commercial real estate. My construction crews can pour three, sometimes four floors of reinforced concrete a day. There's nobody else in Chicago who can do that. We do the finish work and handle the sales and leases. When this pandemic is over, we're going to capitalize all over the Midwest. Anyway, we have judges and lawyers to handle our competition problems now."

Frank didn't want to argue with Vinnie about commercial real estate. Advisors at his bank had told him that Covid-19 had destroyed commercial real estate. Nearly everyone was working from home and the trend only seemed to be growing. "What are you going to do with Helen?"

"Don't worry, Frank, I'm not going to hurt her, but I'm going to put the fear of God into her young partner. We may have to take him down to Grand Cayman to get my money back, but we'll get it one way or another. You started it with the woman. You'll have to finish it."

"Vinnie, I'll pay you back. I've got the money."

"What are you talking about?"

"I've got the money. I have money you don't know about. I'll make good on this."

"Frank, you're being very sly with me about money, and you know I don't like that. Where did you get this money that I don't know about?"

"From the restaurant, Vinnie. We did very well. Angie was a genius with money."

"Then why didn't you invest your own money?"

"My money's tied up in stocks and bonds; it's not as liquid as yours. Anyway, I wanted to make you proud of me—show you I was still with it."

Vinnie was silent. He looked out at the cold autumn mists rising from Lake Michigan and thought about what Frank was saying. This thing with his uncle and the Omaha woman went deeper than he'd thought. That, plus his uncle trying to play the big shot with someone else's money made him reconsider the situation. He waited for Frank to start talking again.

"I'm in love with her, Vinnie. She makes me feel like I didn't think I'd ever feel again."

"You're thinking with the wrong organ."

"I'm not thinking, I'm feeling, Vinnie. I love her...and just so you know—that organ you're talking about doesn't work so well anymore."

Vinnie hesitated again. He hadn't figured on romance complicating what was already a financial debacle for him. He had long assumed that his uncle was mildly demented, but the old man seemed sharper and more animated than he'd remembered.

"Alright, Frank. My assistant will give you an account number. Then she'll take you over to accounting. I'll expect you to wire what you owe me as soon as you get back to St. Louis. I don't care what you do with the woman, but I don't want to hear about her again. She's bad for my business."

As Frank left Vinnie's office, a masked assistant handed him a file and a thumb drive. She took him to the accountants, who explained how to wire money. Frank knew how to wire money, but he listened patiently. He didn't want to make Vinnie even more angry about money.

Frank returned to St. Louis in the same way he had come to Chicago. It was late when he arrived at Beaumont, and only the evening receptionist greeted him. He was too agitated to go to bed. He sat up for several hours trying to think of what to do next. Clearly, he had been conned by Helen and her accomplice. He would have to confront her, but first he had to get the money to Vinnie. Owing money to Vinnie was always a bad idea. He wanted to kick himself for getting sucked into a scheme that now seemed so obvious. He had spent thirty-five years in the restaurant business repelling hucksters proposing wild get-rich ideas over drinks in his bar at midnight, and here he had fallen into a big one himself. He wanted to kick himself even harder for putting Vinnie's money into a scam he should have recognized.

The next morning, Frank drove to his other bank in the suburb of Clayton, the one where he kept his money from the restaurant and his investments. He had earlier called a vice president he knew and arranged a meeting. Banks were always happier to take your deposits than return them, and this was a big withdrawal. The bank official was young, efficient, and attractive. She impolitely questioned his motives and his mental competence. Frank was courteous but firm. He had the balance to cover this withdrawal, and the bank had the money, or claimed it did. Finally, after several hours of wrangling, she contacted their private bank department, and they all agreed to sell some stocks in Frank's portfolio and wire the money to Vinnie's Chicago bank. Frank called one of Vinnie's assistants and told her that the money was coming. He drove back to Beaumont for the larger confrontation—the meeting with Helen that he dreaded. He felt he had Vinnie off his back, but he feared that his love affair with Helen would soon be over.

By that time, it was cocktail hour for the three friends. Their social scene had shifted to Helen's apartment after Charlie's liquor stash had been confiscated by Beaumont's staff. Charlie said it was the new secretary in the business office who had betrayed him. Frank and Helen agreed it was better to have their cocktail hour in a less public venue anyway.

When Frank walked into the reception area, Charlie rushed up to him. "Frank, I'm in trouble. Helen is saying I assaulted her."

"You beat her up?"

"No, she's saying it was sexual. You know me, Frank. My brain may be scrambled, but I wouldn't do anything like that. I'm all about consent."

Frank took Charlie to his apartment. "If she's already filed a complaint, the cops will be here. Just sit down and take it easy. I'll get you a glass of water. Then I'll go talk to her."

After Charlie had calmed down, Frank retrieved Vinnie's file and went to Helen's apartment. When she let him in she immediately burst into tears. "Oh, Frank," she said, "something terrible has happened. Charlie groped me. I think he was trying to rape me."

"Save the dramatics, my dear. You're not on stage. Have a seat and look at this." He handed her the file.

She didn't bother to open it, as if she knew its contents. She looked at Frank and began crying again. "I'm so sorry, Frank. I didn't want it to turn out like this. You must believe me."

"Helen, at this point I won't believe anything you say. You and your young friend conned me out of half a million dollars, but there's something you don't know about me."

Helen lifted her intoxicating eyes to him in apparent confusion and disbelief. She was clearly playing another role, so Frank told her straight what she had gotten into. "I don't know how you and Jeffrey, or whatever his name is, found out about my bank account, but it's not my money. It belongs to Vinnie Palermo, my nephew in Chicago. He's big in the outfit up there, and he knows all about you."

"The outfit?"

"The mob. You stole half a million of mob money. You can sugar up to me, but you have no idea what you're into now."

"We didn't steal it. It's a legitimate investment. The software suite is real."

"Oh, stop it, Helen! Vinnie knows all about you and your young friend. You've taken money from the wrong people this time."

"I was literally starving, Frank. I couldn't get work. All the theaters are closed because of the pandemic. We thought this was a sure thing, that you had so much you wouldn't miss it."

"The only sure thing is you're in big trouble. You'd better tell your boy Jeffrey to contact me and get me the money, or else he's going to get some visits from people he'd rather not meet."

Helen sat in silence—stunned beyond tears. She only emitted an occasional sniffle as she alternately looked at Frank and then studied her clasped hands.

"I'm going back to my apartment, Helen. I thought we had a good thing going, but you ruined it. You'd better think about what you've done and get the money back to me. Don't contact me unless you've done that."

Frank spent the next three days in his apartment. He did not go to the common areas and took his meals in his apartment. Charlie dropped by for reassurance on the first day, and Frank told him only that there would be no consequences from Helen's accusations. When Charlie came by on the second day, he had forgotten the entire matter.

Being alone clarified Frank's thoughts and concentrated his mind. He thought about Helen and what he had lost. He couldn't remember exactly how he had fallen in love with her, but he remembered her beautiful eyes and her commanding presence...and her wonderful hands. Helen had improved his life. He was no longer checking the newspaper obituaries every day. He was sleeping better, and he had regained the weight he had lost after Angie died. Another telling improvement was that since meeting Helen, he hadn't once tried to brush his teeth with his hemorrhoid cream. By the fourth day, he had nearly decided to contact her when he heard a gentle tapping on his door. He saw Helen through the peephole and opened the door.

"Frank, I remember what you said about not wanting to see me, but I have no one else to turn to. Jeffrey has disappeared."

"What do you mean—disappeared?"

"I can't find him. I tried to call him; then I took a cab to his place and his clothes are still there. There's even food in his little refrigerator, but he's disappeared. I can't find him and he doesn't answer on his cell phone."

"He probably got a visit from Vinnie's people and he's lying low for a while."

"Then why won't he answer my calls? And he left all his clothes and shoes--everything. He would never leave all his clothes and shoes.

CHAPTER 5

Frank drove Helen to Jeffrey's apartment. It was in a shabby extended-stay hotel in south St. Louis County near the Mississippi River and south of the interstate beltway. The apartment was what Helen had described—neat and clean with food in the small refrigerator and Jeffrey's clothes hanging undisturbed in the bedroom closet. There were expensive suits, sport coats, and casual clothing with multiple pairs of shoes in shoe trees, all in a precise order. Frank calculated that he had never owned that much clothing in his lifetime. Jeffrey's toiletries were still in the bathroom, also in precise order.

"I think he's just lying low," Frank said. "On the lam as they say. There's no sign of a struggle in here."

"I know Jeffrey better than you do. He would never leave his clothes no matter how big a hurry he was in."

"I'm not sure what we can do. I don't think we want to get the police involved."

That comment drew a frown from Helen. "Why don't you call your nephew? You could ask him if he knows about this."

"You're changing pretty quickly from supplicant to supervisor in this little play of ours."

"I'm sorry...I'm not trying to be bossy. I'm just worried and I'm really frightened. I've never been involved in something like this."

They left the apartment and drove to a fast-food place for coffee. Sitting in Frank's car, drinking their coffee, Frank said, "Before we go any further, I think it's time you came clean about this scheme and how you cooked it up."

Helen sipped her coffee and gathered her thoughts. "I've known him for years. His real name is Jamie Madden. He put some production money into a play we were doing in

Omaha years ago. He's older than he looks. He tried to date me after my second divorce, but he's not my type. I hadn't heard from him in years when he contacted me several months ago about you and your bank account."

"How did he know about the bank account?"

"He didn't say. He just said you had a lot of money in the bank and he had an idea about how to get some of it. He said you had so much money, you'd never miss it. He figured you were impaired and getting money from you would be easy. He'd already picked out the Corbett identity from a Denver obituary he'd seen on the internet."

When Frank didn't reply, she said, "Frank, you have to believe me. I was desperate. I had no money to even put food on the table. All the theaters were dark. I couldn't even get money doing TV commercials. They were looking for younger actors. I know what I did was immoral, but it's hard to be moral when you're hungry."

"Didn't you have savings?"

"I was never good at saving money. My last husband promised me some money, but after he died, I found out he had given all his money to his children from his first marriage. I had nothing. I didn't know where to turn."

"You have no children?"

"There were no children from any of my marriages. I was stupid about that. I didn't want anything to interfere with my acting career. I had big goals and ambitions. Unfortunately, it didn't work out."

"Helen, you've made some mistakes in your life, and your current situation is probably your biggest. But underneath it all, I don't think you're a bad person. I've seen you help people at Beaumont. I was very impressed when you went into the women's restroom to help poor Mrs. Jenkins after her accident. Even the staff didn't want to go in there to clean up that mess."

"I was only doing what was necessary at the time."

"You were doing what nobody else wanted to do." Frank paused and thought about how far he was willing to take this conversation. "As an actress, what roles did you like to play? Besides the one you've been playing recently."

Helen frowned again. "I guess your sarcasm is deserved, and by the way I'm an actor, not an actress. I've always wanted to act. I had some classical training early on, and I tried to do everything from Shakespeare to modern drama. I never liked Shakespeare, and I guess I wasn't very good at it. Most of the women in his plays are either devils or damsels in distress. As for Shakespeare, I think his love sonnets are the best things he wrote. As for me, I've always favored more modern English and American drama. I loved to do plays by Wilde and Shaw."

"You never went to New York?"

"I had some offers, but the circumstances never worked out. Trying to juggle marriage and an acting career was a full-time job. My first two husbands finally gave up on me. Said I wasn't committed enough to marriage. Then my third husband had the nerve to up and die on me. That was over a year ago. By the time his estate was settled, and I learned I was destitute, Covid came along."

"I don't think you're cognitively impaired."

As far as I know I'm perfectly functional, but I was literally in danger of being turned out on the street. Being impaired was another role I had to learn to play."

"Didn't you get some of the government stimulus money?"

"I did, but it wasn't enough. I looked for secretarial work, anything. There was nothing out there during the spring. Everyone was locked down in Omaha. They weren't shooting new TV commercials, just recycling old ones. I used to be a hand model, and they told me I had gotten too old to be a hand model. Nothing was working."

"What about your big scene with Charlie?"

"That was part of the act. Jeffrey coached me. He literally scripted the assault scene with Charlie. He said I needed to be more irrational and unpredictable to be believable as a cognitively impaired person."

Frank was impressed with her ability to shift between fictitious and real names. "After Angie died and I sold the restaurant, my doctors told me I was impaired. But they said depression might be part of it too. They wanted me to take a bunch of medicine. I wouldn't do that, and since I met you, I've been feeling a lot better. Maybe it was depression all along."

"I think it was," Helen said. "So here we are."

"So here we are," Frank replied. "I wonder where we should go from here."

"We could get married."

"I was thinking the same thing."

"I said it first."

"Please forgive me... but are you sure about this?"

"I'm as sure as I've ever been about anything. What about your nephew?"

"We're clear with him. I've paid him back."

"You talked to him?"

"No, but I sent him the money."

"You need to talk to him. You know I'm Jewish?"

"We'll have to find a rabbi and a priest. We don't have much time."

"What do you mean by that?"

Frank knew he had entered a verbal minefield. "I just meant in terms, you know, of the calendar. The holiday season is right around the corner. We need to move along on this."

"You're saying I'm old?"

"I know I'm old. I don't know how old you are, my dear."

"I'm old enough to read you. You don't want to call your nephew, and I think we need to find Jamie."

After considerably more verbal maneuvering, they decided they would get married in the general sense without settling on a date or a venue. Helen said she would try again to contact Jamie, and Frank agreed to call his nephew. In Frank's telephone conversation with Vinnie that afternoon, the nephew professed to know nothing about the apparent disappearance of Helen's accomplice. Vinnie insisted that he had not moved on his threat to retrieve his stolen money, saying he was as puzzled about Jeffrey's disappearance as Frank. Vinnie could not bring himself to mention Helen's name. Helen's attempts to contact Jamie also failed.

News of Frank and Helen's approaching marriage spread through Beaumont like a California wildfire. Frank wasn't certain how it got started, but he did remember telling Charlie that he had proposed to Helen. In the collective memory of Beaumont, which was sparse, no residents had ever married each other. Helen had helped several of the more impaired women there and was genuinely liked. Frank was considered a convenient and necessary prop. Everyone wanted to attend the wedding. Frank thought he had arranged for a simple ceremony by a judge at the county courthouse, followed later by a religious ceremony, but the growing enthusiasm among Beaumont's residents and the restrictions of Covid-19 complicated his plans. County rules prohibited a large gathering, even in an outside venue. Frank began working on a video link between the ceremony, wherever it might be, and Beaumont.

Then Jamie showed up.

CHAPTER 6

Jamie called Helen on her cell phone to report that he was at the bus terminal in downtown St. Louis. Frank had him take a cab to South County Mall, where Frank and Helen would meet him and pay the cab fare. When they connected at the mall, Jamie began babbling in a barely coherent manner about being kidnapped and taken to Grand Cayman, being forced to empty his bank account, almost drowning in the sea, being attacked by strange underwater creatures, trying to get back to the States without money or a passport, and a harrowing bus trip from Miami to St. Louis. He was dressed in a running suit and sneakers and looked and smelled like he hadn't showered in a week.

Helen succeeded in calming him sufficiently to extract a story about thugs entering his apartment in the dead of night and flying him to Grand Cayman in a small jet, where he was walked through a largely non-existent airport private security and put into a car. On arrival at the bank, the thugs forced him to convert the sum of his bank account into a cashier's check. He couldn't remember anything more about the cashier's check. Then two of the thugs had motored him out to sea in a small boat and dumped him into the ocean at midnight. He later learned he had been thrown into a daytime tourist attraction known as stingray city. Apparently, the thugs thought the stingrays would take him out and make it look natural, but the rays were so tame they simply surrounded Jamie as he stood chest-deep in the shallow water. As he waded around in the dark, the rays kept nudging him in expectation of food, which terrified him. He was rescued at dawn by fishermen who took him back to Grand Cayman. The fishermen laughed at him all the way back to land for his naïveté and fear of the rays. With borrowed money wired from a friend in Omaha, he had made his way back to the States and to St. Louis.

Jamie felt he had suffered quite enough for the Frank Palermo caper and wanted only to return to Omaha and never hear from Helen and Frank again. Helen said not so fast. She got a better description of the thugs and directed Frank to call his nephew again. When Frank talked to Vinnie, the nephew maintained that he knew nothing about Jamie's wild story.

"Can you tell me anything about the kidnappers, Frank?" he asked.

"It's hard to get a coherent story out of Jamie, but he did say one of them mentioned that Tony would be happy with the check."

"Now that helps. They're probably talking about Tony Ragusa; he's known as Tony Rags in the outfit. He's kingpin of the waste management arm of the outfit up here. Tony wants to be an oldtimey Chicago hoodlum. His biggest problem is he was born about a century too late for that. His operation is totally different from ours. They're into loan sharking, extortion, and drugs, on top of their waste management empire. Recently they've gone big into healthcare fraud and government stimulus fraud, and I hear they're pretty good at it."

Frank remained uncertain if he believed his nephew, but he recognized a possible explanation for Jamie's story. "How do you think this Tony Ragusa found out about the money?"

"I don't know. Let me do some checking around here. I'll get back to you. In the meantime, keep this Jamie character under wraps. You're talking about the guy you were calling Jeffrey before, right? And be careful. Tony's boys are even dumber than they look. They probably think he's lost at sea. Tony will not be happy when he finds out your boy's alive and well in St. Louis."

Keeping Jamie under wraps was easier said than done. All he wanted to do was collect his clothing, equipment, and credentials, and disappear back to Omaha. Frank pointed out that the people who had kidnapped him would be able to find him anywhere he went. Helen told him they would help him disappear but that he must help them first. She ordered him to forge two passports and driver's licenses for them—showing residences in St. Louis and Omaha. She humored him about his skills and pointed out that he would need his own forged identity papers if he wanted to disappear. Jamie calmed down enough to get to work on his new assignment. Helen had known him as a dapper, supremely confident man of the world. She was amazed at his transformation into a meek and compliant toady.

Frank and Helen were a couple now, and they had taken a suite in the Big Muddy Hotel and Casino complex on the Mississippi River south of the city. Despite Frank's largesse, Helen had insisted that they keep their apartments at Beaumont for the time being. She said she liked 'just in case' scenarios. The hotel suite with its adjacent restaurants was a major improvement over Beaumont, and it still put them close to Palermos. They had offered to take Charlie with them, but he had declined, saying that living next to a casino would be like asking an alcoholic to run a liquor store.

In two days, Vinnie called Frank with more information. "It was Tony Rags, for sure," he said. "Turns out one of my assistants was his kept woman. She knew everything that was happening in my operation, and she was feeding it to Tony. It would have been simple for him to jump in and steal my money. Your girlfriend has started a trend. Now everybody seems to be stealing my money."

"What should we do, Vinnie?"

"Just sit tight. I've plugged the leak here. My assistant is now completely on Tony's payroll. I wouldn't want to be her when Tony's wife finds out about their little arrangement...and she will. I've seen to that. Now I have to figure how to get my money back from Tony."

When Frank put down his phone, Helen said, "We can help him with the money."

"What do you mean?"

"Well, Tony bringing half a million into the country the way he did has to be trouble for him. All we need to do is make him think the IRS and the FBI also know about it. And I think I know how to do that."

"Oh, no. Not another stage show. These people are really dangerous. You don't know Sicilians."

"Actually, I've become quite fond of a few Sicilians I've met. Here's what I think we should do."

Helen laid out her plan to an increasingly skeptical Frank. Before they had a chance to decide on their next move, Vinnie called again. He told them that Tony knew about Jamie's survival and was sending three of his thugs to St. Louis to clean up the mess they had made at Grand Cayman.

Helen said, "We've got to get Jamie out of his apartment now! When they don't find him there, they'll come looking for us. We can hide out in the dementia unit."

"We can do what?" Frank said.

"The dementia unit. We stay in there when the thugs arrive. The other residents will protect us. You're friends with the administrator. She'll help us set this up."

"Why can't we just hire some private security and stay here in our suite? What's wrong with that idea?"

"What's wrong with it is that it keeps us on the defense. We need to start taking this problem to them. We need to make them feel some of our pain starting right now. We can get the county police to arrest Tony's people when they show up at Beaumont, and then we'll take the battle to him in Chicago."

Frank wondered how the pronoun 'we' had become so prominent in Helen's plans. Her scheme sounded dangerous and ill-conceived.

CHAPTER 7

Helen and Frank rushed Jamie out of his apartment along with his equipment and half his clothing. They left sufficient personal effects to be convincing that someone still lived there. Jamie had forged credentials for multiple identities, and Frank put him in another hotel in the county under a different name. They returned to their suite at the casino-hotel complex and cleaned it of any identifying valuables before returning to Beaumont, where with the administrator's permission, they took up temporary residence in the dementia unit. Frank had advanced money to the cash-strapped administrator on several occasions, and she in turn was happy to help the couple with their little scheme. She instructed Barney to help them move into the unit and then to disappear; Barney could intimidate anyone simply with his bulk. The residents of the dementia unit were only told that two residents from the independent living section might be having side effects from an experimental treatment and would be inside the unit for a limited time. As events developed, Helen and Frank's movements were only a few hours ahead of Tony's people.

When the visit of the three thugs to Jamie's old apartment proved fruitless, they went to the casino-hotel complex looking for Helen and Frank. Security personnel at the hotel were less than welcoming, and the Chicago operatives again failed to locate their quarry. They next appeared at Beaumont, posing as two Chicago detectives and a plain-clothes St. Louis County police officer. Since the onset of Covid-19, it was a policy for Beaumont receptionists to photocopy identification of all visitors. Jamie later looked at the photocopied driver's licenses and commented that under different circumstances he could easily get a job forging credentials for Tony. Once in the administrator's office, the threesome produced a search warrant and said they were investigating a fraud case and that Frank and Helen were persons of interest. When told politely that Frank and Helen were absent at the time, they said they would look around anyway. They rang the doorbells of the apartments of Frank and Helen and received no responses. Beaumont's staff would not admit them to individual apartments without permission from the residents, which meant the trio had to be content with checking out the common areas. They did insist on seeing the dementia unit.

Several residents were always clustered inside the locked entrance to the dementia unit. They would greet visitors with comments such as, 'Please help me, I am being held here against my will. If you will contact my family and give them this message, I can get this straightened out and get out of here.' Then they would try to give the visitors handwritten messages to family members.

Imagine the agitation generated by the appearance of three men in suits, said to be from the Chicago and St. Louis County police departments. The excited door watchers followed the visitors around the unit, imploring them for help. The door watchers not only wanted to be released from the dementia unit, they wanted the police to arrest the staff of Beaumont for imprisoning them. Tony's men did not expect to be importuned in this way and had no idea how to react. They had been ordered to scour St. Louis for their quarry, but their reception in the dementia unit caused them to hurry the process and seek a quick exit. Helen was seated with several women at a card table trying to solve a simple jigsaw puzzle. Her shabby dress and vacant look attracted no attention from the three men. Frank was seated on a couch between two men watching an inane daytime quiz show. He also was disheveled and appeared to be dozing with his chin slumped on his chest. Only one of the visitors took a quick second look at Frank and then moved on. Tony's men wanted to be finished with the dementia unit.

When the Chicago crew exited the unit, one of the women sitting at Helen's table said,

"Honey, I hear you're getting married. I'm so happy for you. Is he a nice boy?"

"He's one of the nicest men I've ever met."

"That's him sitting on the couch over there, isn't it?"

"Yes, his name's Frank Palermo."

"I know about him. Well, I hope he deserves you. People living here say you've been very kind to them. We aren't much use in here, but we'll do everything we can to help you."

"You've already done that. Thank you very much. You're all invited to the wedding. We're going to video it into Beaumont."

When Helen and Frank walked to the door to exit the locked unit, all the residents beamed and gave them a round of applause—that is, except for two door watchers who tried to give them messages to their families.

Helen had arranged for Beaumont staff to call the actual St. Louis County police after Tony's threesome entered the complex. The genuine county investigators arrived as Tony's people were trying to leave and quickly exposed the impostors, who were arrested for impersonating police officers and hauled off to the St. Louis County jail. All three of Tony's men had lengthy arrest records and outstanding warrants, which assured their continued residence in the county lockup until they were extradited to Chicago. That was the penultimate time any of Tony's people visited Beaumont.

As soon as Helen knew that Tony's men were out of her way in St. Louis, she set about her plan to take the battle to Tony's operation in Chicago. She put Jamie to work on a Chicago driver's license and official IRS identification papers and badges. Jamie was also able to obtain paperwork on his deposits at the Grand Cayman bank and on the withdrawal, immediate redeposit, and wiring of the money to Tony's account at a Chicago bank.

Helen purchased a women's conservative blue pantsuit and a hooded heavy cloth overcoat at South County Mall. She borrowed a pair of low-cut snow boots from a resident at Beaumont and a relatively new briefcase from Beaumont's administrator. She next launched a diligent internet search on rules for money transfers into the country.

Her efforts exasperated Frank. "I can't believe you're doing this. You're treating this like a melodrama. Don't you realize how dangerous these people can be?"

"I got us into this, and I am going to get us out. Otherwise, we'll never be rid of them."

"They're already looking for you. If they find out who you are, something terrible could happen."

"Don't worry. I can take care of this. I'm an actor, remember?"

Frank avoided describing what 'something terrible' might mean. In his youth, his parents had told him gruesome stories about the Sicilian mafia's methods, and he feared for Helen's life. But when she did a first dress rehearsal as an IRS agent, he was amazed at her transformation. She looked doughty and tough with her faded blue suit, clunky shoes, and a pair of wire-rim glasses. Her hair was tied in a tight bun atop her head, and her beautiful eyes took on a glacial blue tint that seemed to penetrate him when he met her gaze. Frank knew she would have frightened him had she shown up in this guise when he was running his restaurant.

"Stop worrying," she said. "This will move quickly. I'll only go there briefly to plant the seeds of doubt before I put the actual IRS onto them. Nothing will go wrong."

***

October became November. Beaumont was usually a polling place for elections, which was convenient for the residents, but Covid-19 made this impossible. In response to the pandemic, St. Louis County made it easier for residents to vote absentee, but the process was more difficult than simply voting at Beaumont. The situation was further complicated by the intensity of the election—from president, to congressional candidates, to county candidates, initiatives, and referendums. Depending on their degree of cognition, residents tried to learn all they could about the issues and candidates. A lack of understanding, perception, or memory did not hinder residents from having strong opinions, and heated arguments would break out in unlikely places, including the dining room, restrooms, and gym.

Charlie said he liked President Trump, and many women expressed a preference for the

Democrat, Joe Biden. In practice, the residents found it difficult to have ongoing political discussions because of faulty memories, which fueled more anger and frustration. Both Helen and Frank tried to listen without getting involved. When asked their opinions, they had agreed to say only that they would decide before they cast their votes.

"Tell me more about Charlie," Helen said. "He certainly doesn't lack for opinions."

His problem is he can't remember what they are the next day. He's been an oil field roustabout, construction worker, security guard, nightclub bouncer, and school bus driver. He tried to see and do everything."

"How did he wind up here?"

I don't know how many times he's been married, but his wife died about five years ago. When his memory started to fail, there was nobody to take him in. I think he's here on Medicare and Medicaid."

"He seems to consider himself a lothario."

"No thinking to it; he's all of that and more."

"Will you help him vote absentee? It seems like you've been helping everyone else."

"Won't do any good. He doesn't vote; he just gives political opinions. The voting process confuses him."

When the outcome of the presidential election was not decided for several days, residents became more agitated. They wanted closure. By the fourth day, several major news organizations were declaring for the Democrat, Joe Biden. This set Charlie into full rant mode.

"Can't anybody see what's happening? They're dripping in mail-in votes until they win. They're doing it in several states. The fix is in."

Frank and Helen tried to calm Charlie to little avail, and the old ladies didn't help. Mrs. Jenkins and Mrs. McNamara had said all along that Trump wasn't a 'nice man.' He was a 'boor,' a 'TV personality,' who didn't deserve the presidency. They were glad to be rid of him. The country would be a better place without him.

Other old ladies went further. They said Trump was a Nazi and a racist...that he might even be a communist. Everyone knew he had collaborated with Putin. He was probably Putin's lackey.

These accusations enraged Charlie. "You can't be serious," he said. "You have no proof. You're just a bunch of parrots. The Democrats harvested those mail-in ballots in several key states and dribbled them in for days after the election. Didn't you see how the numbers kept increasing for Biden?"

Charlie's opinions only served to make the old ladies more convinced of the certainty of theirs. They also decided it was futile to argue with Charlie and began to refrain from joining the verbal fray. The ladies figured that Charlie was at best just another misguided soul. Their forbearance further agitated Charlie.

"I remember growing up in Georgia," Charlie said. "My daddy told me Gene Talmadge used to campaign by passing out dollar bills and giving everybody a swig of whiskey. The politicians have gotten much smarter these days...except for Biden. His brain is as scrambled as mine, and we elected him President of the United States."

Charlie ranted on until Beaumont's health nurse came to Frank for help. She said Charlie wouldn't take his medications. He was becoming a nuisance, a disturbance. The old ladies were complaining about him. If he didn't calm down, he couldn't stay at Beaumont.

Frank was alarmed because he knew Charlie had no options for alternative living. He suggested they put Charlie's Valium in his tomato juice every morning—just enough to calm him down. This approach made him more docile during the day, but it interfered with his sleep at night. Then they had the brilliant idea of giving him his spiked tomato juice with dinner. Charlie liked tomato juice, and he slept at night and was nearly manageable during the day. Charlie stayed at Beaumont, but he was convinced the election had been stolen from Trump—an opinion he shared loudly and often. He became increasingly vocal again when Trump's lawsuits about voter fraud began to fail in courts in Pennsylvania and elsewhere. The health nurse then had to put Valium in his tomato juice at breakfast and dinner.

"Do you think there's anything to what he's saying?" Helen asked Frank.

"I don't know. I'm not that smart. Sometimes Charlie is a savant; most of the time he's just a forgetful old man. I do think this mail-in voting is a bad idea, especially the way some of the states set it up."

"I think Missouri got it mostly right. It was pretty easy to vote absentee, but you had to jump through some hoops to get a mail-in ballot. By the way, I voted for Trump."

Frank was astonished. "You voted for Trump? I had you figured for a Democrat."

"I am, but I voted for Trump because I thought you were for him."

"I voted for Biden because I figured he was your guy."

They laughed at each other.

"Well, we managed to cancel each other's vote," Helen said. "Maybe we should talk about this before we vote next time."

Chapter 8

The day before Helen left for Chicago, she couriered the documents on the Grand Cayman money transfer to an agent named Betsy McDonnell at the IRS office in Chicago. She had checked the roster of field agents there and had chosen to impersonate McDonnell as a delaying tactic if Tony's people investigated her credentials. Helen was careful to wipe the documents clean of fingerprints and DNA evidence before she mailed them overnight from a facility in south St. Louis City. Helen doubted that the money transfer would conclusively incriminate Tony, but she hoped to arouse enough suspicion to get the IRS looking into the matter. With any luck, a few false moves by Tony might push the matter to a successful conclusion.

Frank had given up on trying to convince her to stay away from Tony's operation. He had begged, pleaded, cajoled, and then he tried to frighten her. He told her grisly tales of the mafia's methods in Sicily and Naples. He had even offered to give her money not to go. She was having none of it. She told him that she was responsible for this debacle and would see it through to the end, whatever that might be. Frank knew enough about the vagaries of her life to marvel at her determination. As far as he could tell, she had never shown such fortitude or singularity of purpose before. He began to wonder about her level of cognition. Without telling Helen, he called Vinnie.

Vinnie listened to Frank's account of Helen's plan and said, "Are you sure about her, Frank? She sounds a little whacko to me."

Frank said he wasn't making up the story and asked Vinnie for help.

"Frank, she'll get herself killed or worse if she's found out. Tony doesn't fool around.

There's a lot of money in play here, and it's not even her money."

Frank stayed with his story and again asked Vinnie for help. "Look, Frank," Vinnie said, "I'm trying to run a legitimate business up here. That's not easy in this town...especially with my name and my background. You're talking romance. I'm talking money...and it's my money anyway. I have ways to get it back that you don't know about."

"I'm sure you do, Vinnie, but I'm really worried about her. Anything you can do to help is important. I've done everything I can think of."

"Alright, Frank. I'll see what I can do. You'd better light a candle and say a prayer for her. And by the way, if she does get into his offices, tell her not to call him Big Tony. She'll find out why."

Helen took a Southwest flight to Midway Airport and cabbed downtown to the IRS field office on Dearborn. After rearranging her appearance in the women's room in the IRS building, she took another cab to Tony's offices in River North. Tony was known to live in an Italianate mansion fronting Lake Michigan just north of downtown, but his office building was a drab steel warehouse in an underdeveloped area along the north branch of the Chicago River. Helen had done her homework and knew where to find him. Tony had a small office for appearances just off Michigan Avenue, but his fortress in River North was the nerve center of his operation. On that day, the dark windowless building seemed to match the weather—cold and foreboding. Two men in heavy overcoats and brown fedoras, pulled down tight against the wind, stood outside the steel entrance door. Helen thought they could have been hoodlums from a century earlier, except they wore white surgical masks and stood six feet apart.

When the cab pulled up, the driver said, "Do you want me to wait for you, ma'am? You're going to have a hard time finding a ride in this area."

Helen thanked him and said she had a ride arranged. She gave him a twenty and told him to keep the change. She then walked resolutely up to the guards at the door, flashed her faux IRS identification, and said she wanted to meet with the accounting department.

They examined her impassively and the IRS identification card hanging on a lanyard around her neck. They checked the contents of her briefcase. Then one produced a cell phone and punched in a number. The heavy metal door buzzed open, and Helen was admitted to a modern lobby with a masked receptionist seated behind a glass partition—a keyboard in front of her, a phone bank and multiple computer screens on either side. Helen showed her identification again and asked to see the head of the accounting department.

"We don't have an accounting department. I can let you talk to someone in the chief financial officer's section." The receptionist photocopied her identification papers.

Helen didn't hesitate. "That will be fine," she said. "This shouldn't take long."

She was shown into a small conference room adjacent to the lobby and took a seat. The room had several surveillance cameras and what looked to be a one-way mirror at the end opposite her. In her short time inside the building, she had already seen several photographs and a painting of a man she assumed was Tony Ragusa. He was small and wizened with a beak nose and hunched features in an oversize double-breasted suit. He was trying to smile in all the photographs, but he had only managed to look menacing. Big Tony was clearly an epithet. She smiled and busied herself arranging her papers on the table.

A masked man came in and introduced himself as an assistant to the chief financial officer. He didn't offer his name or any identification. Helen nodded and began her presentation. "I'm a field agent for the IRS at the Kluczynski Federal Building on Dearborn," she said. "It has come to our attention that personnel with your waste management firm recently transferred a large sum of money from a Cayman Islands bank to an account here in town."

The unnamed man nodded and said nothing.

"You'll be hearing from us in a more formal way, but we wanted to make you aware as soon as possible that you may be in serious violation of federal banking and money-transfer laws." She pushed the papers documenting the transfer toward him, but he made no attempt to pick them up.

"That's really all I have to say," she continued. "It's all documented in these papers I am leaving with you. If you have any questions you can contact me at the number on this card. You'll be hearing more from us soon, probably from the criminal investigation division." She stood and picked up her briefcase.

"You're leaving now?" he inquired.

"Yes, I told your associates that this wouldn't take long."

"Thank you for coming," he said. He escorted her out of the conference room to the building's entrance. "Can I call you a ride?"

"No, thank you. I have a ride waiting."

She walked out into a gray blustery day. Trying not to appear hurried, she turned the corner and sighed in relief when her ride-hailing driver was waiting where they had arranged. Downtown traffic was light in the early afternoon, and the driver quickly arrived at the Kluczynski building. She entered the building and went to the women's room off the reception area where she changed her face and hair back to the appearance of the person known as Helen Cohen. She exited the building fifteen minutes later and hailed a cab for Midway Airport.

Helen was trembling as she found a seat on the Southwest flight to St. Louis. When the plane was airborne, she ordered two small bottles of wine. She took off her mask, and quickly drank them both. The wine steadied her. She was almost satisfied with her little charade, but she wondered if Tony's people had seen through her act. Everything about Tony's headquarters operation had frightened her—from the people, to the décor, to the photographs on the wall. It was a cold, menacing place inhabited by people she never wanted to see again. The experience was enough to make her consider giving up acting.

***

Back at Tony's offices, an assessment was in progress. "I'm sure she was a fake," said the man who had met with her. "Every fed who comes in here is as jumpy as a squirrel in the street. She was as cool as ice." Tony had been watching the visitor through the one-way mirror and nodded in agreement.

"She took a private car to the federal building on Dearborn," said another. "She walked in like she owned the place."

"Her papers and photograph roughly match a field agent there named Betsy McDonnell. She may be legitimate," said a third man.

Tony Ragusa had listened quietly and considered his options before replying. "Fake or not, we may have a problem. The idiots we sent to Grand Cayman should never have deposited the check and wired the money to us. We need to start thinking about how to clean this up. That money may be the lever the feds need to pry us open."

"We could send it back to Vinnie Palermo. Say it was just a misunderstanding...that it was sent to us by mistake...that it was his money to begin with. That could take the heat off for us," said a fourth voice at the table. That fourth voice was Vinnie's mole in Tony's operation. Even as Tony had a mole, Vinnie had a mole of his own, and he had decided to play this card at his uncle's pleading. A mole in Tony's empire was invaluable, but Vinnie also had loyalty to his family. He had instructed his man to make this suggestion. He would find another way to infiltrate Tony's operation.

CHAPTER 9

Helen's return flight to St. Louis arrived after dark, and Frank didn't want to drive to meet her. He hired a limo and was waiting for her outside security. When she came down the corridor, he was elated to see her upright and intact. He embraced her and kissed her enthusiastically.

"You're acting like I've come back from the dead," she said. "Maybe I should take another day trip. There was no need to worry. It was a piece of cake. I was in and out in ten minutes. I only hope I have them second-guessing themselves."

They held hands like teenagers as they walked to the limo. "What's this, a car and driver?" she said. "You're spending money like there's no tomorrow. Can you afford to keep doing this?"

"I have more money than time," Frank said. "Let's get married and figure out how to get away somewhere. I think I have everything planned."

***

As events proceeded in Chicago, Tony Ragusa decided that he had been outsmarted. Two days after Helen's visit to his offices, he had received a letter from the IRS announcing an investigation into his transfer of money from Grand Cayman to his bank in Chicago. The letter informed him that the information had also been forwarded to the FBI and other federal agencies. By this time, Tony had also learned that his putative visitor from the IRS had actually been Helen Cohen, Frank Palermo's girlfriend. He feared she had planted the seeds of destruction in his organization.

"An actress, a goddamn actress from Omaha," he said. "I've been set up by a goddamn actress."

Matters seemed to be spinning out of control for Tony—this check from an offshore bank might bring down his entire business. He called in his advisors, who recommended patience and good lawyering. Tony thought otherwise. He had grown tired of playing defense. He knew he didn't have a good offense, but he thought it was time to try. His few strong-arm operators had been mostly involved in loan-sharking and extortion. He had given up selling drugs on the street because of the unpredictable violence—it was simply too dangerous. Healthcare fraud was a growing income stream for him, but the people he had doing that were of no use in this situation. Most recently he had been working the federal Cares legislation—stealing money with fictitious names and addresses—but he knew that would soon come to an end. His collection people in the extortion game were armed, but they were best at intimidation, not actual violent action. Over the years, his violent criminal operations in Chicago had been so decimated by the FBI that he didn't have actual gunmen anymore. Undaunted, he decided to call four of his most aggressive people together for the St. Louis operation.

Vinnie Palermo knew about Tony Ragusa's plans for revenge, but he found himself in the same predicament. His people were a level or two above Tony's people in the social graces, but they also gave a different meaning to the term 'armed and dangerous'—Vinnie's people were in sales. They were aggressive in closing a real estate deal, but they hadn't been hired for expertise in the violent arts. He did have three men who served as security aides and bodyguards. They were armed, but as far as he knew, they had never fired at another human being. Nevertheless, he called them into his office and told them to get ready for a showdown in St. Louis.

Tony planned to send his people to St. Louis to find Helen Cohen and make her suffer for the impending ruin of his business. Vinnie also was making plans. He had gotten back his half-million dollars in a surprise wire transfer from Tony's bank, which convinced him that Tony was under intense pressure from the feds and maybe from people above them in the outfit as well. Vinnie knew through his mole what Tony was planning, and his plan was to stop Tony's plan, to protect his family—his uncle and even the new girlfriend.

***

Frank and Helen carried off their marriage ceremony. Frank knew an ecumenical Jesuit priest who would marry almost anyone, and the priest in turn knew an unemployed rabbi of dubious provenance from Eastern Europe. This unlikely pair were willing to co-officiate, and their fees were reasonable. They both wanted payment in cash before the ceremony, and they declined invitations to the reception afterward at Beaumont. The ceremony would be in a tavern in south St. Louis City. The tavern had a second-floor meeting room for rent, and Frank had rigged a video feed and paid for a catered meal from Palermos to be served in the dining room at Beaumont. Because of the limits on large gatherings, the residents at Beaumont couldn't attend the ceremony, but they could watch it on the video feed and enjoy a catered meal. Enthusiasm ran high. At the tavern, besides the co-officiants and the happy couple, Charlie, Jamie, and Ms. Jenkins attended in person as witnesses. They all wore masks and maintained an appropriate distance. Only Helen and Frank were allowed to remove their masks for the kiss at the end of the ceremony.

On the day of the wedding, both Tony's and Vinnie's crews drove down to St. Louis from Chicago—about a six-hour trip on Interstate Fifty-Five that seemed to be always under repair. It would have been much faster to fly, but these two groups were bringing arsenals. They had nine-millimeter handguns, assault rifles, and sawed-off shotguns for close work—weapons they had never fired in anger, and rarely in practice. But they came prepared, at least in their minds. Tony's people carried Sig Sauer P320 handguns that had been stolen from a U.S. Army supply depot in south Chicago. Vinnie's people used the Glock 19—a cheaper but entirely serviceable handgun. They knew they had good weapons, but they didn't clean them regularly and rarely practiced shooting at firing ranges.

The wedding of Helen and Frank was a mash-up of Jewish and Roman Catholic traditions. The co-officiants deferred to each other when the ceremony seemed to falter, but at its conclusion everyone agreed that the ceremony had entirely succeeded. It occurred beneath a chuppah, wine was shared, and rings exchanged. Blessings were said, and Frank smashed the ritual glass under his foot. Then the small wedding party removed their masks and shared a bottle of Krug champagne, properly distanced, courtesy of the tavern owner, before returning to Beaumont.

At Beaumont, the wedding banquet was in full swing. The catering service from Palermos had provided copious amounts of food and wine. Beaumont's administrator had relaxed the rule about no alcohol in common areas, and she and her staff stood by anxiously awaiting what might happen. Even the residents in the dementia unit had received the internet video feed and the catered food. Music was piped in over the public address system, and a few residents were feeling amorous and trying to dance in the lounge and library. In a throwback to their youth, Frank and Helen had provided a playlist that included his favorite singing group, Dion and the Belmonts, and her favorite group, The Platters. Frank's all-time favorite song, "A Teenager in Love," was playing when the happy couple entered. The residents greeted the wedding party with spontaneous applause and shouting. At that point, the celebration looked like it would be the high point on Beaumont's social calendar for 2020, perhaps the high point in Beaumont's entire social history.

Then the uninvited visitors from Chicago arrived in the parking lot.

Beaumont's structure was laid out like a horseshoe, with common areas at the center of the building and apartments on either side, surrounding a large central parking lot. Vinnie's crew had made it a point to arrive early and wait, parked unobtrusively in a corner of the lot. When Tony's people arrived and parked near the entrance, Vinnie's crew pulled up parallel to them about three spaces apart. Both parties were in minivans. They had their handguns holstered, but their heavier weapons were stashed behind the back seats of the vehicles. The two groups recognized each other immediately and scrambled out, shooting their handguns wildly and screaming epithets in Italian. Glass shattered in the minivans, in a few nearby vehicles, and in the front entrance to Beaumont. The residents stopped the celebration and hurried to the entrance to check out the noise. When they saw a gunfight erupting in the parking lot, they immediately scattered to their apartments and locked their doors. At the outset, Barney told Beaumont's staff that they were hearing gunfire, and they quickly locked themselves in their offices and called the county police. Barney saw to it that the residents were safely locked in their apartments, and then he locked himself in his bedroom.

As Beaumont's residents scurried for safety, the would-be assailants crouched behind their vehicles and fired around and over and through shattered minivan windows. Luckily for everyone involved, they were terrible marksmen. Their inaccuracy was compounded by the fact that they were unwilling to show their heads and take aim. Great physical damage was done to the minivans, a few nearby vehicles, and the façade of Beaumont, but nobody was even wounded except for a few cuts from flying glass. When the gunmen had emptied their clips, they piled into their minivans, still screaming epithets, and departed in a squeal of tires. The two groups weren't heard from again, and by the time the St. Louis County police arrived, the shooters had crossed the Mississippi River into Illinois. At that point, neither group from Chicago had the stomach to continue the fight.

When the gun smoke cleared, Helen looked at Frank and said, "I can't believe this. What is going on?"

"I think it was Tony and Vinnie's guys. Somebody came down here to teach us a lesson. I think it's time for us to disappear for a little while."

"Well, the bastards ruined our wedding reception. I think it's time for payback."

"You'll think no such thing. Don't you realize the danger we're in? We are going to disappear. That is my first and maybe my last order as your husband."

The St. Louis County police were mystified by what had happened in Beaumont's parking lot. They found empty shell casings and dug a few rounds out of adjacent vehicles and the building façade. There was little additional evidence other than tire markings on the parking lot. The residents couldn't give coherent descriptions of how the mêlée started, proceeded or ended, and no one could really describe the two minivans. What did the shooters look like? Well... they seemed to be middle-aged white men in suits and ties. How many? Maybe ten... no more than twenty. Who were they shooting at? At everything, at each other, at us and at our few cars in the parking lot. Beaumont's staff had no more understanding than the residents of what had happened. Helen and Frank acted as uninformed as the other residents when they talked to the police.

When the police studied Beaumont's surveillance videos, they confirmed that two groups of middle-aged white men had been shooting wildly at each other in the parking lot. They only thing the residents had exaggerated was the number of shooters.

St. Louis was known to be an uncommonly dangerous city—shootings by gangbangers, carjackers, and drug deals gone bad were nightly events. The violence had begun in the city and now seemed to be spreading to the county, but the county police had never heard of a gunfight between white men in suits in the parking lot of a memory care center. They hoped they never would again. It was all deeply puzzling.

When the Illinois State Police found the two bullet-riddled minivans abandoned in the parking lot of a Walmart near the river, there was little additional evidence to be obtained. The minivans and their license plates were stolen, and a thorough scouring of the vehicles proved unhelpful. Upon further reflection, only the St. Louis County police knew where to start this investigation. Tony Ragusa was high on their list of suspects based on the earlier incident at Beaumont.

Chapter 10

After the mêlée at Beaumont, Helen and Frank fled to a small cabin on Lake Carlyle, a man-made lake in Illinois about fifty miles east of St. Louis. Frank had sold the cabin along with his restaurant five years earlier to the buyer and current owner of Palermos. He and Angie had used the cabin on Sundays after Mass for their only day of rest and recreation. He still had a key to the place, and it miraculously opened the front door. They would need to buy more food, but they had brought some of their clothes along with appropriated linens and towels from their hotel suite. Upon settling in, Frank began to consider their situation. Their exit from St. Louis had been frantic—a quick drive from Beaumont after the gunfight to their hotel to gather belongings, and then an even quicker dash across the river to Illinois.

"How long will we need to stay here?" Helen asked.

"I can't say yet. I have to call Vinnie... find out where we stand with him." He could see the fear and anger in her eyes.

Frank drove to the opposite end of Lake Carlyle before placing his cell call. If anyone was listening in, he didn't want to make his location obvious. He talked to Vinnie, and his nephew explained what led to the gunfight in Beaumont's parking lot without divulging the presence of his mole in Tony's organization. Frank was satisfied that Vinnie meant them no harm, but that didn't account for what Tony might do. He drove back to the little cabin, where Helen had prepared a meal.

"I think we're in the clear with Vinnie. He sent some of his people to Beaumont to intercept Tony's crew. That's what happened in the parking lot."

"Thank God none of them could shoot. I've never seen anything like that. What will Tony do now?"

"That's a very good question. He'll likely still be after us. Say... this fish is good. I thought you said you couldn't cook."

"I'm an actor, remember? I can act like a cook."

They ate in silence for several minutes. Then Helen said, "I have to ask you this...I'm not so sure your money all came from the restaurant. I know your restaurant was popular, but I can't account for it being that lucrative."

"Remember I said I was an investor. When I sold the restaurant, I had a lot of free time. I began to study investments. I also followed the trends, and I watched and listened to people. That's always informative."

"What, for instance, could you learn locked up in a building full of demented people?"

"I don't have to remind you that those people at Beaumont are still human beings. You learned that for yourself. I saw you helping them. They took you out of yourself and helped you to help them."

"I grant you that, but what did they teach you about making money?"

"I picked up investment tips from the digital edition of the Wall Street Journal and several other internet services, but I also kept track of what people were doing at Beaumont. Barney helped me with that. He was around the residents every day and saw what was happening, and he told me about it."

"What were they doing?"

"Take Zoom, for instance. We were locked down...couldn't have visitors, and I heard about people using Zoom right and left to see and talk to their families. I heard about that early on and invested."

"And... do you have another for instance?"

"Take Shopify. We couldn't shop for food and other goods, but all around me people were talking about their relatives on the outside using Shopify. I heard that early on, and I invested. There are other examples. Moderna and Plug Power paid off for me."

"I've never heard of some of those stocks."

"You're going to hear a lot more about Moderna very soon. Tesla was another big speculative stock. People have been piling into that one, buying on margin. That's usually a signal that it's time to sell. You have to know what to buy and when to sell. Remember what Yogi Berra said."

"Yogi who?"

"Yogi Berra, the great Yankees catcher...I'm talking baseball. He grew up in St. Louis. He said, 'You can observe a lot by just watching.'"

"That almost makes sense. I don't know much about baseball."

"I'll take you to a game one of these days. I also had investment help from people at my bank. We did very well this year with our finances. That's one good thing that came out of 2020."

"We?"

"You and me. Who else would I be talking about? I also have a separate account that I call play money...money for speculation. Money that I don't mind losing."

"You are definitely not cognitively impaired."

"I think you're right. I think it was severe depression all along. I even had the doctors fooled. They did want me to take medicine for depression, but I wouldn't do it. After Angie died, I got so down I didn't want to live. I finally figured if I was going to keep on going, I'd have to get involved in something. That's when I started learning about money and investments."

"I asked you before. How long do we need to stay here?"

"I think we're safe with Vinnie, but I still don't know about Tony. I wanted to take you five thousand miles away to Italy, and we only made it fifty miles. We can't go to Italy right now with this virus. I'm sorry."

At that moment there was a knock on the cabin door. Frank cautiously approached a small front window and saw a package delivery truck pulling away. He opened the door and picked up a slender envelope. Inside was a deposit receipt from his personal account for five hundred thousand dollars. With it was a note from Vinnie wishing them a happy and long marriage and an apology for not attending their wedding. In a postscript, Vinnie added that Tony was tangled up with the feds about his banking and tax-dodging schemes and probably wouldn't be available for pursuit activities for a good long while.

Frank examined the deposit receipt and said, "I wonder how Vinnie knew we were here?"

"The bigger question is, if he knows, who else knows? I don't think we're safe where we are anymore."

"I think you're right. We probably need to get out of here."

"We could go on the lam, as you say. Spend a year or two on the road with our fake IDs, and you could see if you still want to be married to an actor."

"It's very difficult to really disappear these days. People are too easy to find."

"We have to try, and I want you to know, I worry about your buddy, Charlie."

"Don't worry about Charlie. I never forget my friends. I've already set up a fund for him. He'll be alright. He could move into a nicer place, but I don't think he will. He likes it just where he is. He's got Barney to take care of him and the secretaries in the business office to chase."

"I know a discreet place in Omaha. It's a long-term rental complex where you pay cash, and they don't ask questions."

Frank smiled at Helen's knowledge of the world. "No offense, but a winter in Omaha is not on my bucket list. If we run, let's go someplace warm."

"And you suggest?"

"I think we should try Florida. I always wanted to spend some time there in the winter, but I never had the chance when we had the restaurant."

"Everyone goes there in the winter. I think we'd be pretty obvious."

"I know a guy down there named T.H. He owns a lot of property east of Gainesville. It's pretty rural...around a little town called Interlachen. It's a real quiet place with lots of lakes and a few cabins."

"How do you know him?"

"He came through St. Louis a lot on business. He would come to the restaurant...said he liked our food. I think he's kind of a famous guy. I'm pretty sure he's rich."

"What does T.H. stand for?"

"I don't know. That's what he went by. He always paid cash, so I had no way of knowing much about him. We would sit around the bar late at night over beers and swap stories. He's very personable and he's traveled all over the world. I still have a phone number for him. I'll see if he can help us."

CHAPTER 11

Frank contacted T.H. and made arrangements to rent a cabin on one of the many lakes around Interlachen. They collected their belongings in St. Louis, and Frank obtained a roll of cash from his bank. They drove straight through to Florida, alternating in driving shifts of four hours. In Jacksonville, Frank traded in his car and bought a camper van to satisfy another of Helen's 'just in case' scenarios. It was a cash transaction. They agreed at this point to turn off their cell phones and disable their GPS locators. They then drove about fifty miles south on U.S. 17 along the St. Johns River to the small town of

Palatka before heading fifteen miles west on state road 20 to the even smaller village of Interlachen. In Interlachen, after several wrong turns and no cell phone and GPS aid, they found their way to Lake Susan and an old lakefront cabin that T.H. had rented to them. The place must have been a hundred years old. It was wood-framed with a tin roof, a wrap-around screened porch, and huge windows. The cabin had no air conditioning, but a large attic fan was obviously intended to provide some air movement on hot days. The only heat came from a propane heater in the living room, which almost proved sufficient for the mild winter climate. The property also featured a small dock and a rowboat. Frank found some fishing tackle in the cabin and began to amuse himself trying to catch fish.

"I think I'm beginning to like this place," he told Helen a few days after they arrived. "I checked it out before we left St. Louis, and there are several lakes named Susan in Florida. We can tell people back home we live on Lake Susan in Florida, and that won't help them much."

"This particular Lake Susan is certainly difficult to find. You drove all around this part of Florida before we found it."

Among the fishing tackle was a fly rod and a few dry and wet flies. Frank taught himself to cast with a fly rod and found he could catch panfish by placing a dry fly on the surface among the water grass and lilies near shore and twitching it to imitate an insect. He then began to catch bass by working a wet fly underwater along the front of the grass beds. Bass lurking in the grass would dart out to eat what looked like a small minnow. He rigged an oar over the boat's stern so that he could scull with one hand and troll his wet flies along the grass beds. He crimped his hook barbs and tried to practice catch and release, but a few fish invariably stayed in his boat. In this way a pastime became an obsession. He found several fly-fishing shops in Gainesville and bought a fly-tying kit and began to tie his own flies. There were always enthusiastic fly fishers in the fly shops, who claimed to know what the local fish liked to eat. By the middle of December, he was on the water for most of the daylight hours indulging his new obsession. The weather was mild, and the days were short. They slept at night snuggled under blankets and a comforter that they bought at a Walmart in Palatka.

December's mild weather continued. They would sit on the screened porch after dinner, listening to the gentle sounds of the woods and the lake. One night shortly after dusk, Frank pointed out Jupiter shining brilliantly in the southwest sky with Saturn just visible beside it. He told her that the two planets would appear to converge over the coming days.

"How do you know that?"

"I read about it. It's a Christmas light show for our troubled times."

"I hope you didn't read it on your phone."

"No. I read about it months ago. It's great to be out in the woods on a lake like this. You can really see the night sky."

"I miss the city. There's so much more to do."

"St. Louis, like other cities, is locked down again because of Covid. There's not much more to do there than there is here."

"I still miss it."

"I know you do. We'll get back there soon, but we're safe here, both from Tony and the pandemic."

Their isolation on the lake almost made Christmas irrelevant. One house at the far end of the lake put up some outside Christmas lights, but there was no music, no shopping, no holiday bustle. That absence and the warm weather seemed entirely unlike a Midwestern December.

One night after dinner Helen looked at Frank in the gathering darkness and said, "You mentioning Tony made me think about our wedding reception. Why did you put so much music by Dion and the Belmonts on your playlist?"

"His music was my absolute favorite as a kid. For me it was anything Italian. I liked Frankie Valli too. My parents tried to hide being Italian. All they wanted to do was assimilate. I decided I would be all about being Italian."

"At least you had parents."

"My dad was a bricklayer. He was worn out and disabled by the time he was fifty, but he taught me about hard work. Mom taught me to cook. She gave me all her recipes."

Helen envied Frank for his family. "My mother moved out when I was seven, and my father raised me—in a manner of speaking. He was a schemer and a con man—always had a get-rich plan that never worked out. He wound up in jail several times. I made up stories at school about my dad being a traveling salesman and my mom an invalid. Actually, I was living alone, taking care of myself, when he was locked up. That's where my interest in acting got started—I was acting at an early age."

"I'm beginning to understand where you're coming from. I wondered how you and Jamie started working together."

"I admired him when I knew him years ago. He always seemed to be on top of things—to be successful in his life. That night in the water with the stingrays changed him and opened my eyes. He became a timid, simpering fool. I am very disappointed with him."

"What happened to your mother?"

"She moved to Denver and started a new life—got married and had kids. I visited them several times when I was a kid. She made a nice life for herself, but my life in Omaha was much more interesting. With those visits I did learn enough about Denver firsthand to act like someone who'd actually lived there. As I got older, I began to understand and love my dad even though he was an old reprobate. You have to get a few bruises yourself to feel other people's pain."

"What happened to your dad?"

"I guess he went to jail too many times. I found it difficult to explain his absences to my teachers and the few friends I had. I had to get out of the house and start my own life, and I took an apartment when I was sixteen. I was beginning to make a little money with my acting. I was in a big hurry to grow up and live in the world. Now I find myself in the middle of another strange situation. I feel like a little girl again."

"And your dad?"

"He died about ten years ago—a poor and bitter old man. He never got what he wanted in life."

"What was that?"

"Money and respect, I guess."

Frank could hear Helen sigh in the darkness. "Did you ever see the movie Rome Adventure?" he asked.

"That was an insipid movie. No plot and bad acting."

"It was about romance and young love, my dear. That was the plot, and Rome made it romantic, at least to a young teenager like me. Anyway, there was a song in it called *Al Di La*. Emilio Pericoli sang it in Italian. Troy Donahue played the worldly young guy who explained the lyrics to Suzanne Pleshette, who played the ingenue. I agree with you about Troy Donahue's acting, but Suzanne Pleshette was beautiful—had the best bedroom eyes of any actress anywhere, anytime."

"Actor, darling. She was an actor. And I agree she was beautiful."

"I memorized that song. It inspired me to really learn Italian. It was when I first fell in love with all things Italian. Everything seemed to follow from that—marrying Angie and starting an Italian restaurant...going to Italy every time we had a chance."

"I had The Platters and "Unchained Melody" on my playlist at the reception. I still like that music. I favored songs about romance and being in love when I was a girl."

"You know "Unchained Melody" was originally about a guy in prison, right?"

"There you go with the hard questions again. I liked the song; it spoke to me. Now I like jazz—The Modern Jazz Quartet, Dave Brubeck, and Bob James. So, you see we're both trapped in the past. Do you have any modern tastes?"

"Sure, although it's not exactly modern. I love opera. We have very good opera in St. Louis. That is, until Covid shut it all down. Do you like opera?"

"I can't sing."

"You don't have to sing it to like it. Puccini, Verdi, Rossini, and of course young Mozart, the boy genius. He got the modern era of opera started. I had several arias from *Marriage of Figaro* on my playlist at the reception. *Voi Che Sapete* was playing when the gunfight broke out in the parking lot. I'll never forget that. You can't have an Italian husband and not like opera."

"I'm happy with my Italian husband."

"I sincerely hope so. When we finally get to Milano, I'll take you to La Scala. We'll hear some really good opera. You'll love it."

The busy pace of December and the holidays never reached them on Lake Susan. They had no television, radio, or internet, and they kept their phones turned off with the GPS locators disabled. They celebrated Hanukkah and Christmas in a subdued way, but they had no friends and family to enhance the joy of the season. Frank tried to serenade her with "Have Yourself a Merry Little Christmas," but he couldn't remember all the words.

January of the new year came and went. Frank heard about riots in Washington and on the West Coast when he gassed up the camper van. A new president was inaugurated. All of these events seemed remote and irrelevant to them.

Life in Interlachen proved too quiet for Helen. She obtained a Florida driver's license but found few places to visit. They did get to Gainesville and Jacksonville for an occasional outdoor meal when the weather allowed, but live theater and concerts were still unavailable because of Covid restrictions.

As January proceeded, Helen grew increasingly fractious and anxious. She found no diversions in the cabin, the adjacent lake, or the small village until she decided that she needed a handgun. Frank took her to an outdoor firing range near Jacksonville where she tried out different guns. Walmart had suspended sales of handguns, but at a gun show in Jacksonville she bought two handguns—a Sig Sauer P320 compact nine mm and a big Smith and Wesson .45 caliber handgun. After some preliminary instruction at the gun show, she used her Florida driver's license to access the internet and copy instructions on the maintenance and cleaning of her two weapons at the Palatka public library.

Their location on the lake was so isolated that she could shoot into a hill behind the cabin without disturbing the neighbors. The recoil of the Smith and Wesson proved too much for her, but she grew comfortable with the little Sig Sauer. She practiced shooting from standing and kneeling positions at stationary targets. Frank rigged a moving target powered by a suspended weight with pulleys and cords that she could release. She became proficient at hitting the moving target at 30 feet. Frank was amazed and somewhat alarmed at her dedication to shooting, but he was happy to indulge her new hobby provided he could get away to fish on the far side of the lake while she was practicing.

On his trips to the fly fishing shops in Gainesville, Frank obtained a library card at the public library and checked out financial developments on the internet. He saw an unusual amount of investment activity in late January around several neglected stocks. He had bought substantial positions in Nokia and Blackberry a year earlier on the hunch that these two stocks might take off. He had always thought they were solid companies, although several big hedge funds had been shorting these two and several other stocks for months and boasting about it. He had owned a Blackberry handset in the nineties when they were so popular that they were called 'crackberries.'

Late in January at the Gainesville library he logged onto an internet broker and saw a buying frenzy developing around these two and several other stocks. He sold both positions and directed the proceeds to his bank account in St. Louis.

"I sold a couple of speculative stocks," he told Helen when he returned to the cabin.

"You've been on the internet. I thought we agreed we wouldn't do anything that could be traced to us here."

"I put the profits in a secure account at my bank. I don't think it can be traced to where we are. We did very well on those two stocks."

"I hope you're right about that. At this point I'd rather be alive and poor than rich and dead."

As the corona virus vaccines became available, they each received their two shots. Frank certainly qualified because of his age. Helen qualified with one of her forged driver's licenses. Frank still did not know her actual age, but the age shown on the license made her eligible for the vaccination. Frank heard at the bait and tackle shop in Interlachen that Covid-19 was abating. To Helen and Frank, it was only a rumor.

One perfect sunny day in mid-February, Frank was guiding his boat along the grass beds on the far side of the lake when he saw a black Chrysler 300 sedan pull off the road above him. A man in a dark suit got out and walked down to the shore. "You're Frank Palermo, right?" he said.

"Yes, I am. Who are you?" Frank was ready to jump into the water away from the stranger and use the boat for a shield.

"I'm just a messenger. Mr. Palermo sent me to ask you to stay off the internet. He's afraid someone we both know will find out where you are."

"How does Vinnie know where I am?"

"Like I said, I'm just the messenger. It's Mr. Palermo's business to know things. He's asking you to be more careful and stay off the internet." The man turned and began walking toward his car.

"Why didn't you come to the cabin to tell me this?"

They both could hear the faint popping sounds as Helen took target practice on the far side of the lake. "I think it's safer to talk to you on this side of the lake. Please stay off the internet, *capisci*?" he said as he got into the car.

"*Si, capisco*," Frank said to the departing car.

Frank rowed back to the cabin. He decided that he too would take some target practice. He didn't tell Helen about his encounter with Vinnie's messenger.

In early March, when migratory ducks and geese paused on the lake on their way north, Helen said, "I've had enough," as she gazed at the waterfowl. "I think I'm going crazy here. This isolation is too much. I feel like I fell off the globe. I'd rather go back to St. Louis and take our chances with Tony and his thugs."

"I think we're still safe here."

"I don't care. It's so quiet I can actually hear the sound of my heart beating when I lie in bed at night. I mean I can *hear* my heart beating, not just feel it. It gets really dark here too. The only light is from the moon and the stars. I can even see the Milky Way for the first time in my life. And the snakes...there are snakes everywhere. This place scares me."

"They're just harmless water snakes. They don't have the triangle heads. I sort of like it here. It's quiet and secluded. Hardly anybody bothers you. I'm thinking about asking T.H. if he'll sell us this place."

"Fine! This can be your Florida man-cave. I'm going back to St. Louis if I have to walk. And I never thought I'd say this, but I'm not sure I can ever eat another fish. You've caught so many."

They departed for St. Louis within a week. Frank thought Helen's timing was appropriate. His cash had nearly run out, which meant he would have to begin using credit cards. A lack of cash and the stranger's warning on the lake convinced him that it was time to go. He asked T.H. to consider selling him their little hideaway on Lake Susan. He had grown to love the area around Interlachen. He planned to use the cabin as a fishing camp once he got their affairs settled in St. Louis. He packed some of his fishing gear and Helen her guns. Their clothing was their only other possession. Frank left the blankets and comforter because he hoped to return to the little cabin for the next winter season.

CHAPTER 12

Helen and Frank drove to St. Louis and took their previous penthouse suite at the Big Muddy Casino-Hotel. Helen insisted that Frank keep the camper van as a 'just in case' escape mechanism. Frank insisted that Helen register her arsenal.

"You need to register your guns and get a concealed carry permit. You've got a bra holster, a back holster, and shoulder holster. You're turning into a regular gun moll."

"I'll get around to it," she said. "I need to buy a car, and I want to volunteer at Beaumont."

"I think you need to ditch the Smith and Wesson."

"We can keep it in the van. You never know when we'll need a car gun."

"I'm going to throw it in the river. Neither one of us can handle that big gun. You'll do fine with your little pistol."

"Do what you want. I'll just buy another gun. I need two guns. I also need to find a shooting range to keep my skills up. I've got a lot on my mind. Why don't you invite Charlie over for an evening of poker at the casino? He'd like that."

"Charlie has gambled all his life. I'll bet he hasn't forgotten much about poker. He'll probably win some money."

"Good for him. I hope he does."

Frank called Charlie and arranged for dinner and a night of gambling at the casino. Before picking up his friend, Frank drove down to the river and threw the Smith and Wesson as far out into the swirling water as he could. After cocktails and a steak dinner in the casino's main restaurant, Charlie donned his mask and went to the gaming tables, sitting down to play at one of the two Caribbean stud tables—a game with a progressive jackpot that offered a small chance to win big money. Frank hovered anxiously behind him at first until he was sure that Charlie was comfortable. He then played a few hands of low-stakes blackjack. Helen returned to their suite. Charlie continued to play. The casino staff offered Charlie drinks, which he refused. Charlie was on a hot streak, and his bankroll had grown to about five hundred dollars. Frank returned to Charlie's table and smiled when he saw Charlie's winnings.

"It's getting late, Charlie," Frank said. "Maybe you should quit while you're ahead. I think you need to get back to Beaumont. They'll be worried about you."

"Just one more hand, buddy. Why don't you sit in on this one, and then we'll call it a night."

Frank sat in although he didn't understand the game. The table had three players, Frank, Charlie, and a young Asian man, all masked and appropriately separated. Charlie anted a dollar chip for the progressive jackpot and ten dollars for table stakes. Frank followed Charlie's lead, and the Asian man did the same. The dealer dealt each player five cards down from the automatic shuffler. She dealt herself five cards down and turned up the last card—an ace. The Asian man checked his cards, smiled, and backed his bet. Frank looked at his cards and folded. Charlie checked his cards and pushed out his back bet. He flashed the dealer an admiring smile. The dealer turned up her cards to show a king but nothing else. The ace-king combination put their bets in play. The Asian man had two sevens, which topped the dealer's ace-king. Charlie flipped his cards in triumph—a royal flush in diamonds. He had won the table bets and the long-standing progressive jackpot that had grown to over two hundred and twenty thousand dollars.

Play stopped at the table while overhead surveillance cameras were examined to verify Charlie's hand and the veracity of play. When everything was settled, Charlie had won two hundred twenty-three thousand dollars. He tipped the dealer and Frank two thousand dollars each.

After more delay, the casino management gave Charlie a check for nearly one hundred and forty thousand dollars at about one in the morning, taking out the tax bite before Charlie could collect his winnings. The electronic wall boards in the casino were flashing colored lights and march music was piped in—all for

Charlie. Other players in the gaming area and some staff flocked around Charlie and Frank, snapping photos on their phones and confirming the amount of money in the progressive jackpot. Charlie's story went viral on social media, especially when he told several admirers that he lived at Beaumont. Casino management took photos of Charlie and Frank and a blowup of the winnings check for publicity purposes.

After the hype had finally settled down, Charlie said, "We can go home now, Frank. I'm tired and it's way past my bedtime. I wouldn't have won if you hadn't sat in. The cards fell for me because you were sitting ahead of me."

The next morning, Helen saw the photo of Charlie and Frank on the casino's website and checked postings on Facebook and Instagram. "I hope you understand that our friend Tony will see this too," she said. "You're all over social media. This tells him where to find us. I never thought Charlie would win all that money."

Helen's prediction proved correct. Tony's people alerted him to this development the same day that Helen had learned about it. Tony Ragusa began to fume. "That goddam actress from Omaha is back. I don't know where they hid out, but she's back. I want her taken out."

Sir, we lost them after they left Jacksonville. We don't know where they spent the winter. They just disappeared after Jacksonville."

"You already told me that. What counts is we know where she is now. I want her taken out."

"Sir, you know she's married to Vinnie Palermo's uncle?" said his consigliere.

"I don't care. Vinnie crossed me too, and I don't give a damn about the uncle. I want her taken out. She started all my trouble with the feds and the local cops. They're all over me like fleas on a dog. I've got nothing but clowns around me here. They can't do anything right. Talk to our friends in New York and Miami. Set this up and do it fast while we know where she is."

One of his assistants came back to him within two days. "New York says they can't help us at this time, and Miami says they don't have anyone available in-house. They can recommend two Albanians. They're freelancers working out of Columbia in the drug trade.

They come highly recommended—very fast and efficient—but it will cost us some money."

"Our so-called friends in New York and Miami don't respect me either. I don't care. Just get this done. That woman is poison."

Tony's assistants told him that the two Albanians, Visar and Zamir, wanted fifteen thousand dollars up front and another fifteen after they had killed Helen. If they had to kill Frank, they wanted another ten thousand. The money would be equally divided and wired to two bank accounts in the city of Cali, Columbia. They required Tony to fly them to Chicago, where they would make final plans for the hit in St. Louis. They also required one of Tony's people to drive them to St. Louis. The driver must bring enough cash to buy access to the target for the two hit men. They didn't tell Tony's people how they would do the hit, but by reputation these two shooters were acknowledged to be professionals. Tony said make it happen.

Vinnie got word of this plan through his mole in Tony's organization. He warned Frank and Helen to go into hiding, but Helen adamantly refused to flee again. "Where would we go?" she asked. "We can't just keep running. I've been pushed and pulled by other people all my life. It's time to stand up and be counted. We can take them on. There's only two of them."

Frank was frightened and annoyed. "I didn't marry you for this. It's insane to think we can take on two professional hit men."

"You can leave if you want to. I'm going to stay here and be ready when they come."

Frank inquired about hiring private armed security, but the hotel security people said no firearms were allowed on the premises. If Frank wanted to hire armed security, he and Helen would have to move out and find another hotel.

Without informing hotel security, Helen engaged a security consultant to install a tiny sensor on the suite door that alerted her when the door opened. When activated, the sensor connected to an earbud that played the choral movement of Beethoven's ninth symphony. She planned to activate the system every night when she went to bed. Beethoven was good wake-up music. She also had the consultant install a switch in a corner of the bedroom that activated all the lights in the penthouse, set off two flash bang grenades on the side of the bedroom, and blasted Beethoven's choral movement throughout the suite—all together. She wanted a big surprise for the assailants when they stepped into the bedroom. She slept with the Sig Sauer on her bedside table. Frank saw what she was doing and resigned himself to his fate. He would not run if she was determined to stay.

On the evening of April 14th, Helen and Frank had dinner in their suite. They had heard from Vinnie that the shooters had come to St. Louis two days earlier. It was a leisurely dinner punctuated by banter about their marriage. They shared a Caesar salad and Helen had halibut, Frank a lobster ravioli. They both waxed sentimental and were anxious to reminisce that night. Following their after-dinner decaf espressos, Frank sipped a glass of vino santo. Helen abstained.

"When your nefarious scheme to defraud me fell apart, what made you begin to love me?" Frank asked.

"Neither of us can take credit for any righteous motivation at that time. You wanted my body, and I wanted your money. It's all best forgotten."

"I love your body, but what I needed was companionship. You gave that to me. I also saw the good person underneath your lying and cheating."

"I love the way you balance things, but you're right. Beaumont made me see other people; I mean really see them. My life had always been about me. My talent, my beauty, my profession. The women at Beaumont needed my help, and I found I could give it to them."

"I saw that. You're like Mother Teresa."

"How so?"

"Rich people here and in Europe were always asking her if they could come volunteer in her orphanage in Calcutta. Build up credit in heaven, I guess. She told them something like, 'You want to help someone, help people around you. Start with the person nearest you.'"

"There you go. I fell for you gradually. You were kind to me, and I saw you slipping money to the administrator at Beaumont and to Charlie. I know the old ladies drove you crazy, but I also saw that in the end your heart ruled your mind. That place would have gone under if it hadn't been for you. The pandemic was raging, and people were dying. Nobody was moving in. By the way...I've never told you I love you."

"I know that."

"I've been genteel poor all my life. Unless you're on top of the pile, an actor doesn't make much money. My marriages didn't work out, and my last relationship was an unmitigated disaster. He was long on promises and absent on production. Then the pandemic hit, and everything shut down."

Helen smiled and said, "I'll bet you have never been hungry...really hungry."

"No...we always had food on the table. We ran a restaurant. We had enough frozen tomato sauce and meatballs to last a lifetime. Our marinara sauce with calamari was famous."

"That's what I'm saying. When you get really hungry you begin to think desperate thoughts. I was eating at a soup kitchen when Jamie came along with his wild idea to steal your money. He had a little money to set up his plan, and I had nobody else to turn to. I had already sold most of my furniture. I was about to lose my apartment; it was my last hold on a reasonable life."

Conversation about food, money, and saints continued until near bedtime. Helen sent Frank to the small bedroom they had rented one floor below. Returning to the penthouse, she checked her setup and formed two lumps with pillows below the covers. She lay awake reading beside the lump on the right until fatigue finally overcame her. She had a foreboding that trouble would arrive before dawn. She plugged the door alarm earbud into her right ear and chambered a round in the Sig Sauer before putting it on her bedside table. Then she, too, dozed off.

***

After two days of surveillance, Visar and Zamir decided to make their move. They walked into the deserted hotel lobby at 3 a.m. The magnetic keycard to Frank and Helen's suite lay in a sleeve atop the front desk as arranged by Tony's driver with a substantial payment to the night desk attendant. Visar pocketed the keycard and followed Zamir into the back room, looking for the desk attendant. Finding the room empty, they walked quickly to the unisex bathroom at the back of the room and tried the handle. The bathroom door was locked.

"Please come out, sir," Visar said. "We just want to thank you for your help."

Zamir motioned to Visar and pointed to the empty lobby. "We skip him," he whispered. "He's never seen us. Let's get the job done."

They took the stairwell to the penthouse floor, where they used the keycard to enter Frank and Helen's suite. They checked the door and door-jam for sensors and found nothing. Now they were ready—night vision glasses on, their Ruger MK II weapons in their hands and the Sig Sauers jammed under their belts.

Helen awakened to the entrance alarm music in her ear, picked up the Sig Sauer, and moved to a chair in the corner of the bedroom. Visar and Zamir padded across the dark living/ dining room and paused at the bedroom door. They raised their weapons and nodded to each other. As they opened the door and stepped into the room, Helen activated her sound and light show.

She saw the two shooters pause, temporarily stunned by the flash-bangs, light, and music. She gripped the Sig Sauer with both hands and shouted in as deep a voice as she could summon, "Drop your weapons and freeze. You are under arrest."

Visar and Zamir were disoriented. They dropped their Ruger weapons, and Visar turned his head in the smoke toward the unseen voice. He saw Helen sitting in the corner and immediately reached for the Sig Sauer in his belt.

Helen saw they both were wearing body armor over their torsos. She squeezed off two rounds into Visar's right shoulder as he turned. Visar howled and dropped his Sig Sauer. He fell to his knees, clutching his shoulder. Helen pointed her gun at Zamir and told him to remove his Sig Sauer with his left hand and place it on the floor. Then she told him to move away from the gun and sit quietly on the floor facing her.

Frank was the first one to arrive. "What the hell happened? Are you okay?"

"I just shot that man over there, darling," Helen replied. "Please back out and wait for security."

Frank remained in the doorway. "Shouldn't we call an ambulance?"

Security will do that. Let's just keep these two boys quiet until they get here."

Security did exactly that. They placed plastic handcuffs on both assailants and wrapped a compression bandage around Visar's shattered shoulder. The county police were not far behind hotel security and took control of the scene.

By dawn, the assailants had been hauled off, and the county police had finished their preliminary investigation. They took multiple photographs and tagged and removed a significant amount of evidence, including Helen's Sig Sauer.

At 9 a.m., Helen and Frank were sitting in their dining room eating a late breakfast. Helen took a sip of cappuccino. "See, I told you," she said. "The cops took my gun. Now I'm going to have to buy two guns."

"You saw this coming, didn't you?"

"I had a hunch, an inkling. I am never going to be passive again. I am going to be an actor on a larger stage now. I am going to fight to protect my new life and the people I love. I asked for this strength and I got it."

Music was playing on Frank's small player. It was "Heart and Soul." He smiled at Helen. "Do you recognize this song?"

"It was the tune that was playing when we first met. I remember it."

"I put together a playlist of my parents' favorite songs. I guess we all become our parents in the end."

"I hope that's not true in my case."

Despite the shock and confusion of the night, Frank was pensive. "You know there was another saint named Teresa," he said. "She lived in Spain a long time ago. She said something about more tears have been shed over prayers answered than over prayers unanswered."

"I know who she is. I tried to play her in a short piece years ago. I was terribly miscast—a cynical Jewish girl playing a Roman Catholic saint. By the way...I do love you. I hope you understand that."

"You love me in spite of me being just plain vanilla?"

"Darling, you are much more than plain vanilla, and I do love you. You must believe that."

"My dear, you'll get no argument here."

About the Author

Thomas Morgan is Thomas Morgan Hyers, a practicing pulmonologist in St. Louis. He is in the same age group as the principal characters in the story, and he experienced the year 2020 in his medical practice and in his personal interactions with family and friends. He currently practices pulmonary occupational medicine and conducts clinical research with new pharmaceuticals. He wrote this story during the peak lockdown period when his practice was curtailed by Covid-19. In addition to his medical responsibilities and writing efforts, he likes to spend time with his family, garden and cook.

Thanks for reading! Please add a short review online where you purchased your copy, and let me know what you thought!

Turn the page ... for a sneak peek

... the story continues

Marinated Money

Chapter 1

The late spring of 2021 brought relaxation of Covid-19 social restrictions in St. Louis. The mask mandate was dropped for fully vaccinated people, which meant it was effectively dropped for everyone. Social distancing was less strict, and more people were allowed into sports events, bars and restaurants. However, some people found it difficult to give up their masks; indoor and outdoor events were marked by masked and unmasked people mingling and talking in close proximity. Helen Cohen Palermo and Frank Palermo gave up their masks but kept their distance from crowds. They continued to reside at the Big Muddy Hotel and Casino and to take most of their meals in their suite.

Three weeks after Helen had shot one hired killer and disarmed the other, Rex Raulerson, the manager of the hotel and casino complex, summoned Frank to his office. "Thank you for coming, Mr. Palermo. How is your wife?" He asked behind his mask when Frank took a seat.

Frank noticed Raulerson's mask was decorated with dollar signs and diamonds. "She's fine. The whole thing was a shock to her, but she's doing well."

"I'm glad to hear that. It was a shocking incident. I hope you understand how much we are concerned for her."

"Yes, I appreciate that. I'll tell her about your concern." Frank figured Raulerson had more on his mind.

"What I wanted to say is that the shooting was difficult for all of us...for the hotel staff and all of our guests. The police have cleared her, I assume?"

Frank smiled at the rhetorical question. "Yes, they said it was self-defense and brought no charges about the unregistered gun although they confiscated it."

"I'm so glad to hear that. You know we don't allow firearms in the complex."

"It was your night desk guy who let the shooters into our suite."

"We have corrected that. He's no longer with us...but that's not what I wanted to talk about."

"What is it you wanted to talk about?" Frank had disliked Raulerson from previous meetings, and his distaste for the man was growing by the minute.

"Mr. Palermo, the long and short of it is that I'm afraid that you can no longer stay here. I'm sorry to say that, but we have to uphold our reputation."

"Your reputation?"

"Yes...we are a family-oriented establishment. We cater to that demographic."

"For the love of Pete, you run a freaking casino."

"Yes, but we are trying to cultivate a family atmosphere."

Frank laughed. "You've got prostitutes in the bars and parking lots."

"We are in the process of correcting that situation.

"So...let me be sure I understand this. You want us to move out because you think we are polluting your family atmosphere?"

"We would appreciate that."

Frank smiled at Raulerson's response and thanked him for his candor. Frank said he would talk to Helen about the matter. He rose and returned to his suite. When he entered, Helen said, "What was that all about?"

"They want us to move out."

"Why? What did he say?"

"He basically said it's because you're shooting people."

"Darling, those two were trying to kill us, and I only shot one of them. And he's likely to recover although he's going to have to learn to shoot with his other hand."

"I pointed that out to Raulerson, but it didn't seem to matter. I also think he's still mad about Charlie winning all that money at the tables."

"Maybe I should talk to him."

"Helen, my dear, I doubt that would help. He's mortally afraid of you already. I think we should find a house somewhere on the river and be done with these hotel people. Anyway, I'm tired of their cooking."

Helen considered the possibilities before agreeing with him. "Maybe you're right. We're too obvious here. We need a place with more security. By the way, I bought two new guns."

"I hope you registered them this time."

"Not yet, but I will. They'll be perfectly legal."

Frank wondered at Helen's continued disregard for the law and rules of polite society. "I'll start looking for a place," he said. "You really must register your guns before something else happens."

"Good. I think somewhere south on the Mississippi or maybe on the Missouri overlooking the wine country. We're going to need some private security." Helen's smile indicated her distain for requests about her guns.

"I like the Missouri out near St. Albans," Frank said. "They already have security for some places out there. We could work with them. There's a high bluff I know about with beautiful views of the river and the valley."

Frank set about his assignment. He found a spacious house with a guesthouse on ample acreage above the small village of St. Albans—about 40 miles west of St. Louis. The house featured a panoramic view of the Missouri River as it wound its way south and east to join the Mississippi above

St. Louis. He commissioned an agent to close on the house under an LLC he had created. Frank dreaded his notoriety brought on by the shooting. Keeping a low profile had changed from a preferred lifestyle to a necessity for him.

When the sale closed, he established a security perimeter around the house with movement-sensitive lighting and alarms, and he signed a contract with a security company that served a gated community in St. Albans. Frank recognized that in the public eye he was a wealthy man. He needed a bodyguard with a physical presence but also with the intelligence to run the technology that he had installed. In his mind that person was Barney Browning, the nursing aide at Beaumont. He knew Barney had worked in private security before taking the job at Beaumont during the financial meltdown in 2008.

When Frank offered him the job, Barney said, "Thank you, Mr. Palermo. You know I've been at Beaumont for over 10 years. I'll have to think about it."

"So... it's Mr. Palermo now. What happened to plain old Frank?"

"The Frank I knew at Beaumont was a good man who was struggling with the loss of his wife.

The Mr. Palermo I know now turns out to be a very wealthy man—wealthy beyond my imagination."

"Barney, I have confidence in your imagination. I'm offering you one hundred fifty thousand dollars, the guest house, and a large expense account."

"Like I said, Mr. Palermo, I'll have to think about it. I'd also like to talk to Ms. Palermo."

"Why Ms. Palermo?"

"I'd be working for both of you. I'd like to hear her take on this."

***

Helen met Barney after she had finished her shift as a volunteer in Beaumont's dementia unit. She was seated at the conference table in the library when he entered. He took a seat at the other end, near the entrance. His size made the conference table look small.

"It's good to see you, Ms. Palermo. The residents have missed you. We've all missed you."

"Thank you, Barney. You wanted to talk to me?"

"Mr. Palermo has offered me a job. I'm sure you know that. I want to be sure you agree with that idea."

"We talked about it, and I'm fully on board. We bought a home out near St. Albans, and we need a security coordinator."

"What do you really know about me, Ms. Palermo?"

Helen hesitated. She recognized that she was now being interviewed. "I know I like you. You've taken good care of us when we were at Beaumont. I think you're competent and honest."

"Let me just tell you a few things about me. My family has been in this country a long time. We're descended from slaves who were brought over from Benin a long time ago. When my ancestors bought our freedom, which was long before the Civil War, we took the name Brown. It's a common name among people of color because we didn't want to use the name of our owners. In the late 19th Century, we changed our name to Browning, after the gun manufacturer. For people of color to legally change the family name wasn't easy in those days, but we did it."

Helen was uncertain where this conversation was going, but she decided to hear him out. "Thank you, Barney," she said. "I didn't know that."

"Let me tell you something about your family, Ms. Palermo. You are descended from a family of New England shipbuilders and financiers. Your ancestors owned some of the ships that brought my ancestors to America."

Helen was temporarily at a loss for words. "I knew my mother's family came from New England, but I didn't know we were shipbuilders. Barney, how do you know that?"

"We have to know things about people. It's how we have survived. In the old days we passed this information by letters and word of mouth. Now it's much easier with the internet."

Helen feared that Barney wouldn't take the job. "Where does that leave us, Barney?"

"I think it leaves us where we started. I wanted you to know something about me before I took the job. I like you and Frank. You're both good people, and I think that history from centuries ago should stay there and not always be dragged into the present."

"Thank you, Barney. I look forward to working with you. Do you mind if I tell Frank about our conversation?"

"I hope you do. I'm happy to move on from here with our present understanding."

Helen realized that Barney had seized permanent moral superiority with their brief conversation. "Can you tell me more about your family?" she asked.

"My family story will have to wait for another time. I have to get back to work. Thank you again for your time." With that Barney rose, signaling that the interview was over.

Helen marveled that what she had thought was a routine job interview had become a revelatory event for her. When she returned to her car, she phoned Frank and told him about the interview.

Frank laughed. "That sounds like Barney. He always knows things that surprise you, but don't underestimate him. He's the only staff member at Beaumont who knew all our faults and failings and still tried to help us."

"Why don't you just give him some money. You've got plenty to spare. He makes me a little uneasy."

"He makes everybody a little uneasy. Part of that is his bulk; I make him about six feet eight and 300 pounds. But there's something else about him that's hard to describe. Even at half his size, he'd still be a formidable person. I can tell you one thing. When you need him, he'll be there for you."

<hr>

MARINATED MONEY

A Helen and Frank story

by

Thomas Morgan

Fall 2021

www.ingramcontent.com/pod-product-compliance
Lightning Source LLC
Chambersburg PA
CBHW070358200726
48294CB00003B/978